Searching for Safehavens

Ezra Ellenbogen

Text copyright © 2019 Ezra Ellenbogen

Jacket design by Vikncharlie from Fiverr

ISBN: 9781793927026

Printed in the United States of America
January 2019

First Edition

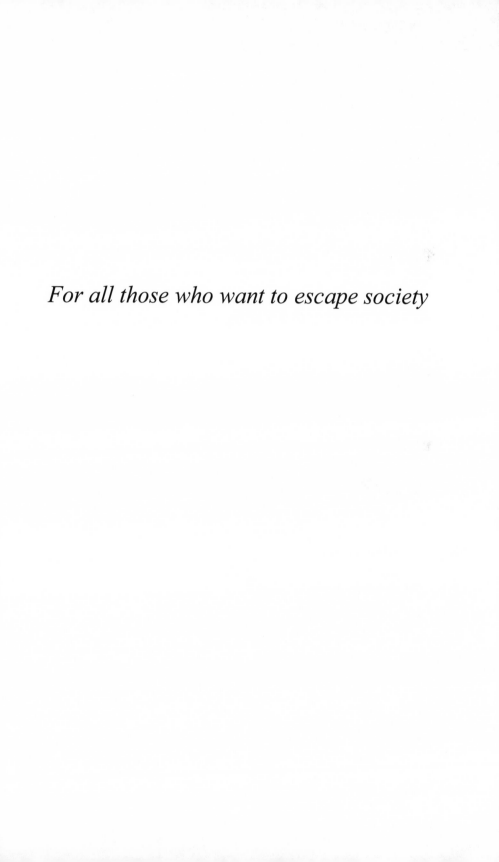

For all those who want to escape society

Chapter One

In 2027, the world experienced a nuclear fallout. DC and Beijing fought back and forth, and eventually involved Paris, London, and Jerusalem. The world population declined from eight-point-two billion to a mere three-point-six billion. After DC, Beijing, Paris, London, and Jerusalem started fighting back and forth, Islamabad and New Delhi joined in. Moscow was excluded, as they had gone through a major economic collapse earlier in 2021. There were no sides in this war; it was everyone against everyone. Many major cities were destroyed by the thousands of nuclear weapons involved in the war. Juneau, San Francisco, Phoenix, NYC, DC, London, Cambridge, Paris, Nantes, Berlin, Rome, Riyadh, Mumbai, New Delhi, Islamabad, and Karachi were all destroyed by the nuclear fallout. Yes, that sounds like a lot, but, at the time, it was predicted that almost every country's capital would be destroyed. That was also when the DC Virus spread, which was caused by radiation. Nuclear weapons were banned after the nuclear fallout. Beijing stood tall at the end of the day. BRICS started expanding due to that power, and Brazil left a year afterward.

Then, after a mess with Alaska that left Canada in shambles, the African Economic Collapse decimated what was left of the African economy in 2033. China also just straight up bought ASEAN in 2034. Turkey started expanding and Sicily seceded, and it was around this point everyone knew the world was engulfed in chaos. After leaving BRICS, the Brazilian economy relapsed in 2039. Due to a lack of agriculture around the world, the Uruguayan Influenza started spreading in 2042. The continent of Africa went to war with itself in 2044. Then, in 2047, the Bosnian Kingdom reformed but was overshadowed by the formation of a Neo-Soviet Empire in 2048.

Then, after the Soviet expansion, the Warsaw Incident occurred. The Warsaw Incident was when the Neo-Soviet Empire surrounded Warsaw and resorted to nuclear weapons. To combat this illegal behavior, Beijing started spreading a controlled virus in eastern Soviet Russia. This virus didn't stay controlled for long. The Warsaw Virus spread nationwide. Soviet Russia collapsed, Japan collapsed, and parts of China collapsed due to the spread of the Warsaw Virus. The Taiwanese government took advantage and started rapidly expanding and involved itself in a war with eastern Asia that lasted until 2076. In 2060, the African continent entirely and absolutely collapsed.

Meanwhile, the Neo-Ottoman Empire continued expanding. They had reached as far west as Kosovo and as far east as Pakistan. They used the same classes and dynasties as the days of old in the original Ottoman state. Not so far away, France started colonizing excessively. In 2070, South America economically collapsed. In North America, a major war was being fought to control the future of the continent. Between the newly colonization-obsessed Alaska, the Neo-French Empire that had colonized every bit of Earth they could, the remnants of the United States, and the Central-American Alliance. This war ended in a surprising American victory in 2084, but the other states involved were puppeted and later released in 2085.

In 2078, after the rapid Taiwanese expansion, some idiots decided to dig up the only remaining remnants of the plague that were stuck in permafrost in Svalbard. The Norwegian Plague was spread and all of Scandinavia collapsed in 2079. The two major world powers left, the Neo-Ottoman Empire and the Asian Taiwanese Dynasty went to war in 2081 in Tajikistan. The Ottoman Empire had colonized India fully at this point. Then, the US decided to get involved with the Taiwanese Dynasty in Western Alaska.

Right now, it's 2091. My name is Austin. I live in Eden Prairie, Minnesota, which is right outside of Minneapolis. I was born in Austin, Texas in 2070, hence my name, to a large and idiotic family. I was born with a severe case of Uruguayan Influenza due to my lack of a proper processing system for the new and chaotic world's air. My family hates me for it. They loved Austin, and never missed the chance to point out the only reason we moved was that my medicine needed for the Uruguayan Influenza is only in the US north of Nevada. We could've moved to Ohio, but medicinal centers weren't in Ohio at that point. Medicinal Centers are only in major cities, of which there are few left.

There are thirteen major cities in the US left. At this point, "major cities" are cities that are populated with over seven-hundred-seventy-thousand people. That is a high bar at this point. Denver is the largest city in the US. The major cities in the US are Angelo (formerly Los Angeles), Reno, Boise, Tucson, Denver, Dallas, Austin, Jackson, Minneapolis, St. Paul, Toledo, Cleveland, and Anchorage. Worldwide, the US has a low population. Many of its cities have less than half the population of cities in China or Europe. Internationally, Shanghai, Beijing, and Istanbul have the highest populations of cities. Beijing is as populated as the entire country of Chile. Istanbul is almost as populous as Beijing but is behind by forty-eight-thousand people.

It's 2091, and the entire world is in absolute chaos. Everyone in my family hates me. I'm writing this so someone in the future can see what it's like in 2091. I would love to escape one day. Today, my family went to the city to get our medicine for the month. Minneapolis is just a hop away. We do not have a car or anything, so my family walks in a large group. Luckily, no one sees us, as living in a world with such a small population, there's about one house per thirty-four miles, except in the major cities. Minneapolis is a fairly bustling city, and traffic is expected. Cars are uncommon nowadays, as the world economy collapses, the prices of cars and other things steadily rise. It's been a dream of my family to get a car, as it would make it easy to move. In order to move to Eden Prairie, we had to hitchhike through six fairly large states.

As we walked to the city, there was a bit of conversation. It's interesting to wonder how language has changed since 2020. Lots of slang I know today seems to be from the 2030s or 2050s. Not many "new languages" have arisen in the 2000s. However, many languages have been changed so greatly or combined, to the point where they are unrecognizable. In the recently Ottoman conquered northern India, there are a few composite languages like Hindi Turkish, Turkish Urdu, and Turkish Sanskrit.

So many languages have been lost. Latin was the first known "dead" language. Japanese is absolutely dead. Almost every non-major language in Africa is dead. Languages vary by state or country. Most countries still exclusively speak their original official language. However, in the US, most states do not speak English fully. Louisiana French Creole and Tagalog are the only languages used in Louisiana and has spread to southern Arkansas. In northern states, German is mainly spoken. Yupik is used in Alaska. Tagalog is a popular language in Western states. My family speaks German, Hmong, and Vietnamese in order to communicate with others in the state and nearby states. Hmong is the main language in Minnesota. German is a very common language in every state, and Vietnamese is common in the south, where we used to live. My third sister speaks Dakota, Arabic, and Chinese as well. I am currently trying to learn English, as English is still somewhat spoken worldwide. Literally, about one-hundred percent of the world's population is multilingual. It's simply just a necessary skill in this crazy world. I can not really learn languages that well, as nobody in my family talks to me.

Anyway, on our walk to Minneapolis, we conversed (whilst excluding me) and snacked on breakfast tubes. Yeah, breakfast and other meals or snacks are condensed into tubes of food or juices. They actually taste pretty good and it negates the use for silverware or cutlery. There are many different flavors, such as Strawberry and Sugary Breakfast Cereal. They are nutritionally sound and they are very cheap. Rich people still use regular food. It's ridiculous and expensive.

On our walk, we noticed the transition between the city and the fields. The city is filled with large, wooden buildings. Almost every building is a "skyscraper." The tallest building in the world is in Chengdu, China. It is a shrine to the second artificial moon. It is a metallic beast in the center of the countryside. Buildings are almost always taller than mountains, as space is sold by the square footage of the land it's on, not by square area of the building. Many buildings are very thin so that they are able to be stacked right next to each other. It seems pointless, as there is so much untouched area in the countryside. It almost looks like the Dutch architecture of old. Many hotels are stacked up wooden hotel room pods.

Whilst the buildings in the city look tall, thin, and futuristic, my family's house in the countryside is short and stout. We mainly farm tomatoes and the land we own is about thirty-four acres of farmland. While that may seem large, it is relatively medium-sized or average sized compared to other major farmers' farmland. Tomatoes are still a very profitable crop; others include sugar and beets. Our barn has seventeen bedrooms, fourteen for the children (including me), two for my parents, and one guest room. It is a very spacious area for the small number of children we have, but we're looking to expand. That many children may seem like too many, but it is required by law to have a certain number of kids in order to properly repair the decimated world population. The law varies by country or state. In Minnesota, the minimum is twelve. There is never a maximum. In the Taihoku region of Taiwan, the minimum is eighteen, the highest in the world. In stark contrast, the minimum in Denmark is a mere four children.

As I was saying, on our walk to the city, we saw the transition between the city and countryside along with many new stores. Wow, I sidetrack a lot. We saw many new stores, as Minneapolis's population recently surpassed one million. This qualifies for the next level of a major city. There are many tiers. At seven-hundred-seventy-thousand, you are first considered a major city. At eight-hundred-forty-thousand, you are considered a population center. At one million, you are considered a major population center. At one-million-five-hundred-thousand, you are a supercity. The few remaining supercities include Beijing, Shanghai, Istanbul, Taipei, and Keelung. As of November 2091, Minneapolis is a major population center. St. Paul is still a major city, with its population at eight-hundred-thirty-thousand.

At each tier of a major city, new stores are installed. The major medicinal pharmacies are some of the main companies that regulate investment in cities based on their tier. Hotel, motel, and apartment companies are entirely regulated by the tier of the city. These companies only expand once the population per hotel has reached a maximum. Most other companies are considered commodities and are regulated based on the amount needs of the area. With the new growth of Minneapolis, many new pharmacies, hotels, and commodity shops showed up. In the downtown, a new apartment complex stack was built up. It has one-hundred-seventeen rooms stacked side by side upwards. The newer hotel, motel, and apartment complexes are slowly inching south towards our property. We had talked about leasing out unused property to a major hotel company. A few new medicinal pharmacies have shown up, with many having competitive prices. Luckily, nineteen new convenience stores have come about. To complement that, a toy store and five dollar stores have shown up. We got some new flavor meal tubes while in the city. I am excited to try "Generic School Pizza."

Once we got to the city, we could feel it. The bustle and hustle of the streets and the bright light and loud cacophonies emanating out of suspicious dollar stores and convenience stores, the ticking of the clock in the city center, and the shouts of desperate advertisements begging for our attention. Drones flew overhead, buzzing past our ears. It's nothing compared to the hustle and bustle of cities in Asia.

We started our monthly shopping trip at one of the new "budget" medicinal pharmacies. We got two months' worth of medicine for everyone except me, for their medicine was on sale. Meanwhile, I was the only one whose illness is different. My medicine is considerably more expensive than others. When walking out, my father and my sixth sister went behind the building. I had noticed this behavior happening before, but this time I followed closely behind. Many people are drawn in to buy narcotics from the companies marketed under the promise of satisfaction in this desolate world, and my sixth sister and my father are two of those many people. I didn't bust them; they would've killed me if I did. The large companies take advantage of helpless populations that visit medicinal pharmacies for needed

8

medicine (which is almost everyone) by selling them narcotics and then reporting them and winning money in court. These companies' behavior makes me sick.

Afterward, we went to a major convenience store and bought some meal and snack tubes for the month. We got some great new flavors. After we had some lunch, we went back to the wagons to grab this month's crops. All of my sisters had brought wagons full of tomatoes. We didn't sell our seventeen pounds of tomatoes for as much as we would've liked to, but we reached a decent amount. However, we realized that we had three extra pounds since they didn't have enough room to keep all seventeen pounds. We went to another convenience store and sold the remnants. Since it was a new convenience store, they had absolutely no clue how much to pay per pound and we tricked them into giving us twenty-two percent more than the precedent. This was quite the surprise, so we decided to shop around at the new dollar store with our newfound cash. A dollar store is self-explanatory. Everything in the store is a dollar. The only reason ridiculously budget stores like these are even able to exist is that producers will sell things in such bulk quantities, that it will be cheaper to make.

The dollar store was quite something. It was about half the size of regular convenience stores and smelled atrocious. Many of the things being sold were made of plastic and looked and felt cheap. They also had a few small snack tubes, which were somewhat scary considering how cheap they were. We ended up getting a few trinkets, I got an Eiffel Tower look-alike statuette, and my sisters and brothers got little statues as well. It's surprising how much they were able to sell for one dollar.

Thus arises the subject of currency. There is no generally accepted currency, but most areas have three to eight different accepted currencies. This is because many currencies are very similar, such as one American Dollar to one Canadian Dollar. No new currencies were invented since the South Sudanese Pound. Many old currencies are used, since no country has the budget to constantly produce new currencies, except the Taiwanese Dynasty in Asia. The Taiwanese Dynasty continues to print money, even though it is detrimental to their budget. They continue to because they strive to be unique and seemingly richer than any other place in the world. It may seem confusing, but it's not. You just use any old currencies, and most times you combine the use of both in one payment. That's why most areas use currencies that have similar conversion rates, as to avoid confusion. For instance, in Minnesota, the currencies used are USD, CAD, BMD, EUR, GBP, BSD, and AUD. Those are all of the very common currencies to be used. Bosnia uses the BAM, AWG, BZD, BBD, and NLG. Extensive research is done to determine which currencies can be used in an area.

So we started to walk by, and by this time the day was practically over. Everyone in my family was tired, especially me. It had been quite the day of walking around the city. I wonder what it must be like to actually live in one of those cities. It must be hard with all the people, just everywhere. I couldn't imagine living in Denver, I've seen pictures. In a place like that with a decent state flag, you'll see it everywhere. The flag of Minnesota however, is absolutely horrible. It hasn't been changed since 1893!

Flags nowadays are different from days past. Almost every country has changed their flag and the flag of their regions, except the US. Even with its new allies and territories, the US cannot be bothered to change a single one of their flags. Many flags have been changed nonetheless. The French flag is now a bends flag (similar to the flag of the long-dead country of Tanzania) with its iconic colors and the words printed diagonally: "Le Pouvoir Du Peuple," meaning: "The Power Of The People."

We noticed the transition between city and countryside yet again as we strode home. The walk felt longer than on the way here. Once we got home to our old-fashioned house, we decided to play a game. Of course, I was not included. I went to bed as my family's talk of "Tám đến bàn tay của đại lý." I sat, sleepless, in my bed for hours, like most other nights, the thought of the world as it scares me to a point where I can not sleep.

It was 12:42 at night. I still could not sleep. My fifteen assorted relatives were all fast asleep. Meanwhile, I was thinking about how to escape. It's no secret that I've always wanted to leave Minnesota or even the US. Life is better literally anywhere else, for I do not have to be with a family that hates me and excludes me.

Denver would be fun. I could live in a hotel pod and work at one of their infamously unnecessary hair salons. It is ludicrous that people will pay to have their hair styled. They could be spending that money on supplies for their family or themselves. Also, the climate is much more temperate in Denver. It would be fun to live in Hong Kong, with the mix of the British culture from the invasion, the Chinese culture from the reintegration, the Japanese culture from the brief imperial colonization, and the Taiwanese culture from their takeover of the island and ones surrounding. Plane tickets are expensive, so if I was going to move, I would either need to hitchhike or somehow get my hands on a large amount of money. Flights in 2091 cost almost two point four times as much as they used to, and then there are the fees, and then there are all of the new rules and regulations. It would be quite the hassle, but that will never stop me.

I want to find a safehaven. Someplace where the messed-up rules of modern society do not exist. Someplace where I can actually be free and where I can actually enjoy life. I want to actually achieve something with my life. I do not want to be yet another schmoe from Austin who dies at seventy-six due to forgetting medicine for the Uruguayan Influenza. I do not want to just be yet another person in the vast population, I want to change up this desolate world, to make it better, or, to find a new one.

It's not like there is a new society just a twenty-five-hour plane ride away from here. If there is, how would I know? There isn't a library anywhere in the US that hasn't been turned into a museum. There are some in Europe, and there are a ton of religion-exclusive ones in Asia. The libraries in the US were wiped out in the dumbing down of America and also through the dozens of wars they've fought. There isn't a way I could find a map or atlas. The world map is so complex nowadays, that most map-making companies just gave up. If I was to find an atlas, it would be outdated. The last maps made were in 2035. I have a plethora of reasons to doubt that a country that seems isolated enough from the rest of the world to have its own unique, functioning society in 2035 would still exist fifty-five years later.

Maybe this is a safehaven. Maybe I just do not appreciate it. I have a roof over my head and a family to provide for me. I live near a major population center and I'm properly fed and medicated. Maybe all major cities are safehavens. Major cities are mainly inhabited by rich people who can afford to live there. If I lived in a major city, then I would live in a safehaven, for I would be rich and isolated from society. Alas, maybe growing up, making a fortune, and moving to Denver would be right for me.

Well, despite the odds, I am still going to try. I am going to try and sneak out and fly to an isolated society. I will try my darndest and I hope to escape from my horrible family no matter what. I will get a job in Minneapolis, with all the new stores, they're likely to need new employees. Maybe a worker or customer there will tell me where a safehaven is. I will save up, even if it takes years. However, if it's a safehaven entirely removed from society, the flights may be cheap considering how few people would go there.

I am decided. In the morning I will walk to the city and apply for a job. Despite not being the oldest, or being even close, I will be one of the only two people (including me) with a job outside of our family's farm. Maybe this will make my parents respect me, maybe this will make my siblings respect me.

I walk downstairs to our language library. We have a small room with eighty dictionaries in it. It is not unusual for a family to have eighty dictionaries. Many families will try and learn as many languages as possible in order to communicate with as many people as possible. I picked up one of the English dictionaries and went to the kitchen to grab a snack tube. I snacked as I tried to learn English.

English is a very odd language. Words like pony and bologna rhyme and words like cough, though, rough, through do not. It is very hard to learn because sometimes things are silent and then there are words like myriad and their, there, and they're. There are myriad ways you can screw up your grammar in sentences. Semicolons are ridiculous; they have no use in modern English.

I hope to learn English, as it will be useful for getting a job at a store. However, it might be odd if someone in Minnesota didn't already speak Hmong. I am decided, I will get a job, and I will purchase a flight to a safehaven. But first, I must find a safehaven. There must be at least one safehaven left in this miserable, desolate, depressing world. I will escape my horrid family and find a good place left in the world, no matter how long it takes.

I woke up and walked downstairs, as usual, I was last. I sat at the bar-like table, grabbed a sugary donut tube, and waited for my father. And waited. And waited. And waited. He didn't show. My sisters and brothers started to notice. My mother slowly came down the stairs with bloodshot eyes and bags under her eyes, everyone gradually quieted as she motioned for us to be quiet.

"Children, f-father has passed. He was sold illegal drugs that were not medicinal, but recreational. He was sold them under the precedent they would have no effects on his life, they had lied in order to gain a small amount of profit." my mother shakily said.

Chapter Two

The spectacle of the invasion rivaled that of the many invasions before when this city was known as Constantinople and Byzantium. The ground shook as the Greeks rushed in shouting their war cry. The cacophony was quite annoying while I was trying to read. I worried not, for the Greeks had come many times, and yet it doesn't seem like Istanbul is Greek territory. The measly Greek army would never rival the might of the Neo-Ottoman Empire! We had collapsed before, and we will learn from our many mistakes. The Neo-Ottoman Empire started in 2037, and the world hasn't been the same since then. We have expanded as far north past Crimea, as far south as Riyadh, as far east as the Indian front and as far west as Serbia. We have made an alliance with many countries, including the Neo-French Empire, Bosnia, Bosnian Herzegovina, and the German Empire. The Balkans are a mess, but soon the Neo-Ottoman Empire will conquer them all (except the Bosnia-Herzegovina region).

Alas, I have not introduced myself. I am Maurie. I was born in Istanbul in 2067 to the Ottoman royal family. I live near what used to be the Bosphorus in a grand Ottoman castle with classic Turkish architectural design. Yes, we are the descendants of the House Of Osman. We are a country that is constantly at war. Before I get too far into Neo-Ottoman history, I should let you know I am writing this for a school assignment. I am supposed to journal my thoughts throughout the weeks. It is quite the dishonorable assignment.

The Ottoman Reconquista occurred in 2037 when the House Of Osman finally regained control of the Turkish government after the mess with Erdogan and his ancestors. You might ask why someone would try and reestablish a long-lost empire that failed while it existed, and to that, I would answer that one would do so in order to regain control of a larger area since the country in question is able to provide for the populations, and to spread Islam yet again. The way the Neo-Ottoman Empire has gotten so bloody rich is through strategic war investments. The UN is just a joke, no one would support the UN task force, as there is no direct benefit for those who do so. Since the Reconquista, the Neo-Ottoman Empire has invested in its allies' wars and turned a profit through an alliance. Since 2037, the Neo-Ottoman Empire has been involved in many wars that do not directly include them.

Also, the Neo-Ottoman Empire was responsible for the Bosnian reformation and is paid yearly through funding by Bosnia and Bosnian Herzegovina. During the Bosnian reformation, the Neo-Ottoman Empire invaded the war-torn area and puppeted the governments of the area. For two years, the Neo-Ottoman Empire supported the entire country of Bosnia and Herzegovina. Then, they reformed the government into three parts: The Kingdom Of Bosnia, The Bosnian Republic of Herzegovina, and The SRPSKA Free State; the last of which was eventually integrated into the Neo-French Empire through a request.

Our alliances have made us the strongest country on Earth, yet we are facing many threats. The Indian front was originally between the Indian

Tribal government and the Neo-Ottoman Empire, yet since the Taiwanese reconquered the area, it has been a proxy war over India. The Taiwanese Dynasty is not a force to be reckoned with, yet they are a force who has no allies. They are quite the lucky country, as they have only expanded so much because of the collapse of all of the countries around them due to the Warsaw Incident.

We are currently in many wars. To the north, we are fighting a war with the Ukrainian Confederacy over southern Ukraine. In the south, we are fighting the Mecca front in order to regain control over all of the Islamic population. In the west, we are fighting against Greek and Serbian rebels. In the east, there is the Indian front against the Taiwanese Dynasty. In 2089, the Ottomans officially regained full control over the Indian subcontinent, and they are fighting to keep it that way. In 2090, the semi-independent republic of Alaska waged war against the Taiwanese Dynasty over a few islands in the Bering Sea. It seems like the odds of the Neo-Ottoman Empire winning over the Taiwanese Dynasty are exactly fifty-fifty. It is quite the nerve-racking war in my opinion.

It's fun watching the game of war play out in front of your house. It almost like a chess match. Each piece is set up with an assigned move, and the king is the main target. In this case, the king was me. I am the current heir to the throne and there is not another immediate heir for sixteen generations. As many assassins have come to know, it is wise to kill the heirs first, so that once the sultan is gone, no one can replace him or her. My father is currently the sultan of the Neo-Ottoman Empire. My mother died before I was born.

A pawn moved forward two spaces. They are now at a stand-off with another pawn. The pawn who was on the offensive was Greek, and it made sense considering the stupidity of the move. It seems that the Greek rebellion is an ideocracy at this point. Well, the Ottoman pawn calls for backup, the Greek pawn does nothing. Then, a bishop moves in on the other end. Ottoman pawns start gradually moving forward, yet ignoring the standoff. The Greek bishop fumbles around. Greece is losing pawns left and right, and the last Ottoman pawn has come forward from its hiding spot right in front of my castle. The last Greek pawn falls. Greece only has a rook protecting the king, and a knight precariously placed to somewhat protect the queen. Also, they have the bishop. The bishop moved closer to my castle. What was happening? I'll tell you what. A Greek bishop was about to take the Ottoman king. These weren't chess pieces, this was real life and I was in danger!

I threw my book to the ground and fled. The first shot fired. The Greeks had found a way to create an electronic cannon that broke the sound barrier. Those damn inventive Greeks! My ears rang with the sound of the Ottoman army losing. I had left the room by the time it exploded. I stumbled, feeling the sudden headache from the sound barrier being broken. My ears rang, and I was too weak to hear, see, or anticipate the next shot. The cannon screamed with the sound of Greek rage that they had been holding on to since the beginning of time. The Greeks had won once before, and they wouldn't win again. The next shot hit me like a bomb. The searing pain in my chest was complemented by constant pangs later. I was blown back to the end of the hall, as I saw the remnants of the upper floor of my castle.

I scrambled around and ran down the stairs. The third shot came, this time from the king. It was much more powerful. Luckily, it missed. I tumbled down the stairs and ran to the door, but made sure to grab my key. There was no use in locking the door, as the entire mansion would be blown up by the Greeks. I ran throughout town and across markets to a "sewer" door that was two miles away. I unlocked the door with my key and hopped in. It wasn't a sewer entrance. It was the entrance to the underground part of the fire warning. In Istanbul, when an invasion is imminent or happening, one of royal descent or of official status must light a large fire in one of the underground cellars (you light the bottom of the wood and the fire is visible from the street) and others will do so until the warning gets to the sultan. It is a technique adopted from ancient China. And no, a bypasser cannot randomly light the fire, as the wood is surrounded by a fireproof glass enclosure.

I took a second to take a deep breath and regain what was left of my hearing capabilities. This had never happened before; luckily I had a plan for when it did. I lit the fire and ran to the nearby corner of the cellar. I had hidden peasant clothes there months before to prepare for a moment like this. I changed as quickly as I possibly could and nonchalantly rushed out of the cellar and locked it behind me. I was wearing a fez and a baggy and worn salvar.

I ran to the main castle, sprinting by many of those who I could've helped. If the Greeks saw me with a gun, even as a peasant, I'd be an immediate threat and they would kill me. I was out of breath by the time I got to my father's building. I was too late. I had referred to myself as the king, yet I was only the queen, and when they thought I disappeared, they went straight for the actual king. There was not a single moving thing under the myriad of debris. His mansion was gone, and with it, the House Of Osman. I had failed.

If only I had gone directly to his building, but no, I had to worry about myself and get myself a disguise. Boy, I was selfish. My father was dead. The Greeks had won. There was no command in the Neo-Ottoman Empire anymore. It was, quite literally, anarchy. That was if I didn't step up and claim the throne. The House Of Osman's righteous reign has ended, and our depressing fate has befallen us. We gave up, and it was all my fault. I could've telegrammed father. I could've actually thought about it before leaving my castle to burn at the hands of the Greeks. I looked back, I could see my castle's remains from there. How had the buildings burnt so fast? Greek fire.

I stood there, dumbfounded at the sight of a collapsed empire. We would be able to make no advances or retreats without someone in command, and yet, if I stepped up, I wouldn't know what to do. I've spent too much of my life reading fiction and not enough time planning for war.

The Greeks had conquered Istanbul and destroyed the House Of Osman, again. What would I do? My family's empire had fallen and it was my fault. I had to do something, but secretively. Or, I could do nothing, and people would think I died in my castle. The latter option sounded better. Also, I had a couple wads of assorted cash to use at my will. Could I pretend to be an everyday citizen in a barbarically ideocratic Greek society? You betcha.

I waltzed into the hotel looking like a disgraceful vagrant. I had made sure to separate my money into different types of currencies. I had exchanged all of my unusable cash for different currencies at the city's ATM. I slid up to the desk and gathered my confidence.

"How can I help you?" the lady asked, entirely disregarding me.

"I would like a room, a room for permanent stay," I said, trying to sound not like a stuck-up royal Ottoman princess.

The worker scoffed at my appearance and looked through a book of information "We have one room available on the seventeenth floor, although it may be a bit pricey."

"How "pricey?" I asked like a peasant

"Around one-thousand-six-hundred-eight liras a week, or around one-thousand-thirty-seven manats," she said, and then laughed.

I slammed approximately five-thousand-six-hundred-sixty-five Serbian Dinars and five-hundred-thirty-four Saudi Riyals on her desk "Will this cover it?"

Trying to act relatively composed at the sight of that much money in cash, but miserably failing, she shakily replied: "I'll have to check, but I think that's enough."

Twenty-three minutes later, the lady looked back up. She had counted out the money.

"That seems to cover it," she said matter-of-factly.

"Wonderful, may I have the key?" I asked.

She handed me the room key with the number seventeen-seventeen on it. I picked up my luggage and hauled myself and it up the stairs. After a walk that seemed much too long, I ended up on the seventeenth floor. I strode down the corridor and went to the room. Luckily, the key wasn't fake, and it worked. The room was nice but much too small for the price. I dropped my burdensome luggage and started to unpack.

It has been six days since the Greek victory. Six days. That was a long time without an update regarding who actually owned Istanbul/ the entire Neo-Ottoman State. I know that the Greek rebellion had some sort of leader, his name was Qamar Gabris. However he wasn't the founder, Dimos Vassallos could take the claim for that. Dimos was still alive, but he had disagreed with Qamar about how to run a Greek Empire. Dimos was a diehard democratic extremist and Qamar was an ideocratic ideologue. It seems Qamar had the people's support. There were other major Greek rebellious figures, such as the military director Antonis Melis and the war strategist Nikolas Dellis. Other figures included the governor of Athens, Thalis Pappas, the Greek supremacist Trifonas Ballas, and even the Anti-Ottoman Republican liberal Minas Mattas. None of them were female.

Still, even though there were myriad people who could be the new sultan or king, it hadn't been announced. You could tell the entire city was on the edge of its seat. As soon as I started thinking about who would be picked, a commotion arose. I rushed down the stairs and out the door. I looked to someone nearby for an explanation, and they said that the new king was announcing himself and his policies in the town center. People rushed to see who it was.

I followed the crowds and ended up in the town center. There was someone on the stage with a microphone. The crowd was incredibly large and I could barely see who was on stage. I hopped up. It was Qamar. I had predicted Qamar would be the new ruler under his own dynasty.

"Hello, you're all probably wondering who the new leader of Istanbul/ the entirety of the Neo-Ottoman Empire is. It's not me." Qamar announced.

The crowd gasped as Qamar said "I know, it's a surprise. We had an election throughout mainland Greece, and, well, Dimos won."

An old man walked on the stage and introduced himself "I am Dimos Vassallos, I was the founder of the Greek rebellion. I won the election unexpectedly, for the entirety of Greece seems to know the proper way to run a country," he glared menacingly at Qamar, "and I will reinstitute a proper democracy into the shambles of the Neo-Ottoman Empire."

The crowd shuffled uncomfortably as Dimos continued "The Neo-Ottoman Empire had a flawed government, and it was only a matter of time before they entirely collapsed. They had no rulers except for a sultan and an heir, who lived less than three miles away. You think a fully organized Greek rebellion couldn't kill two people in a giant, frivolous, and incredibly easy-to-spot mansions? Face it, you all have no ruler. The Neo-Ottoman Empire has failed"

It was at this point, the crowd starting protesting, and the newly-instated Greek police force held them back. Dimos continued his speech "With the new Greek democracy, we will have a government with a branch of government for every properly controlled region or major population. The list of administrative regions is as follows. Greece, Serbia, Montenegro, Albania, Macedonia, and Kosovo will form the Greek Administrative region. Romania, Bulgaria, southern Moldova, the Georgian Territories, and Crimea will form the Black Sea Administrative Region. Turkey, Cyprus, Syria, Lebanon, Israel, Palestine, and Jordan will form the Turkish administrative Region."

The crowds started shouting and actively protesting. Dimos raised his voice over the crowds "The Saudi Territories, Kuwait, Qatar, Bahrain, the UAE, and western Iran will form the Saudi Administrative Region. Finally, eastern Iran, Turkmenistan, the Uzbek Territories, Afghanistan, Pakistan, and the Indian Territories will form the Indian Administrative Region. There will be a representative from each region, so five in total. They will all meet in the capital, which is now Athens, every month to vote on parliamentary issues. Each region has a different amount of votes based on population. For every vote a region has, they will have a representative to actually cast the vote. The Greek Administrative Region will have six votes, the Black Sea Administrative Region will have three votes, the Turkish Administrative Region will have one vote, the Saudi Administrative Region will have three votes, and the Indian Administrative Region will have four votes. There will be seventeen votes in total."

The crowd went ballistic. Some real stuff was about to go down. "Calm down, you can not resist, the Greek Democracy is in charge! Respect your newfound leaders! Heil the Greek Empire that shall forever live!" That did not help the situation de-escalate even a tiny bit. Dimos saluted to the armed Greek troops in the back of the actively protesting crowd. They started to move in on those who were protesting. Everyone was running amuck. Among the commotion, Dimos shouted a final statement, "**THE GREEK LEGACY SHALL LIVE FOREVER!**" That was the last thing he said before I shot him.

Chapter Three

It was the first day of my new afterschool job at a convenience store. So far, I have made such a small amount of money, that, at this rate, I will have enough money to find a safehaven by March eighth, 2157. I have not found a safehaven yet. Yet. The job is okay, but the customer interaction is hard. The majority of the people come in without making a single noise and pay, and somehow, in some messed up way, some people come into the convenience store looking for a ninety-minute respectful conversation. Alas, people get pretty annoyed if you refuse to respond to them telling you about their meaningless and mind-numbingly boring day.

Oh yes, I forgot to mention that my father is dead. That happened. I didn't know him very well, and the parts of him I knew, I did not like a bit. He was sold illegal drugs and was too stupid to realize they would kill him. I do not really care. On the other hand, all of my siblings are taking it very hard. Mainly, because it allows them to skip school, as our mother is too sad to enforce any rules. My sixth sister took it the worst, but she didn't stop buying drugs, I can see her go behind the alley and come away from it as high as America's debt. It's just depressing. Oh well, I never liked her either, well the parts of her I did know.

Anyway, I hope to find another job or two to fill in the amount of money I need. I could work at a nearby library museum in St. Paul. I forgot to explain that many libraries have been made into museums, meaning you can not actually access the books, which defeats the purpose of it. It is a museum to show off the architecture and types of books that were in use decades ago. They're insanely boring and I can not think of one reason why anyone would go there by their own will in their sane mind. It's preposterously highly priced and the museums still manage to barely make any money. So, I might get a job there as a tour guide, or a janitor. Anything to save up money.

At the convenience store, I've seen more currencies than I ever could've imagined! As I said before, in Minnesota, the currencies used are USD, CAD, BMD, EUR, GBP, BSD, and AUD. Out of those, I've obviously gotten USD the most, with CAD being a close second, which makes sense considering how close we are to the border. By the way, the US-Canadian border has stayed untouched, for the US has just puppeted the entire government of Canada. They're quite the burden, to be honest. BMD is the third most used, which surprised me, but it makes sense considering its astonishingly close exchange rate to USD. Besides the regular and accepted currencies, I've seen others. It has been pretty awkward telling people that Minnesota state law doesn't accept any currency besides USD, CAD, BMD, EUR, GBP, BSD, and AUD.

I've seen some crazy currencies. One guy went to the store with his girlfriend and brought along one-hundred-eighty-five-thousand-eighty-five "Uzbekistani Soms." He spoke with a heavy Russian accent and didn't speak any language I spoke, I had to call in my manager for help. My manager ended up just sending the couple away. They were understandably disgruntled. One young girl brought in seven "Aruban Florins" and only spoke Dutch. I had a coworker who I knew spoke Dutch. The two got in a heated argument and the girl ended up storming away. Too bad she didn't get her little keychain.

Yesterday, a full grown man came in and tried to pay in one-thousand-seven- hundred-forty "West African CFA Francs." He spoke fluent German and he had said that he "found them" in his basement one day. I wonder what one-thousand-seven- hundred-forty "West African CFA Francs" were doing hiding in his basement.

I've also met a plethora of people who speak obscure languages, but one stood out. A non-gendered person came in around maybe five, six days ago and spoke seventeen different languages! Can you believe that? I only speak three and a half languages! The second most languages I've known a person to speak is my third sister, who speaks German, Hmong, Vietnamese, Arabic, Dakota, and Chinese. That's considered too many languages already, and this person spoke seventeen different languages! There are only so many languages you can learn.

I got into a great discussion with him, and he explained to me why he knew so many different languages. He knows English, German, Hmong, Vietnamese, Chinese, Arabic, Dakota, French, Louisiana French Creole, Traditional French Creole, Spanish, Yupik, Tagalog, Haitian Creole, Hebrew, Inuktitut, and Greek. He learned German, English, Hmong, and Vietnamese because they are all common languages where we live. In states near Minnesota, Dakota, Arabic, and Chinese are common along with languages in Minnesota, so he learned those. He learned all the different

French dialects because he lived in southern Louisiana growing up and commonly vacationed to Haiti, where he learned Haitian Creole. He was raised Jewish, so he knows Hebrew. He's an American pharmaceutical salesman and has been across the country thanks to his job. He learned Spanish, Yupik, and Tagalog for that reason. He learned Greek because he wants to move there someday. Finally, he learned Inuktitut because he once met a nice tribe member in Minneapolis who had traveled here from Nunavut and wanted to be his translator.

Yeah, that was a fun day. I wasted the majority of my time talking to a nice person who knew far too many languages. Today, there has not been much business. I've had eight customers throughout six hours and they all were the non-talkative type. It's been a boring day and I can not wait to go home.

My first sister came in a minute or two after I finished writing that. She was quite angry.

She stormed in and yelled, "Who do you think you are staying out this late? What time do you think it is?"

I glanced at a clock, it was 10:49 PM, "Sorry, geez, I didn't look at the time. Normally, you do not even notice me when I am gone."

"Well I do not care where you are no matter what, but our mother is worried sick! She lost her husband and she does NOT want to lose someone else. Get home, immediately!"

"Kay, fine, just let me close up shop."

"You'd better close up shop faster than you've ever closed up shop in your life. I am not going to get in trouble with mom for your idiotic and irresponsible behaviors! You are twenty-one. Act like it for once!

"Twenty-two. I'm twenty-two."

"What? Why in God's good name does that matter?"

"The day dad died was my birthday. I didn't want to celebrate after such bad news. I was just saying."

"Not important. I couldn't give a flying fig about you or your problems! We have to get home before I get in trouble."

"Fine." I put my coat on and gave up. I lied about my birthday, by the way, just to see if anyone would remember. Obviously, they did not remember. I do not care. I do not even know when my birthday is anymore.

"Where were you two?" is what my mother said as a greeting to us as we got home.

"I was just getting my stupid and irresponsible older brother. I can not get in trouble for THAT."

"I just didn't know the time," I said sheepishly.

31

My mother sighed, "Sydney, go to your room and get some sleep. Tomorrow's a school day."

Sydney promptly went upstairs to her room, only after rolling her eyes all the way back into her head.

"Austin, I'll let it go because it's your birthday tomorrow. I hope your job is going well and I'm proud that you're supporting yourself."

"Whaddya mean?" I said like an absolute fool.

"What, it is your birthday in a day. Congrats, you're a day away from twenty-two. Just please go to bed, Austin."

"I'm surprised you even know my name."

"Austin, I just do not talk to you because you are the only child I have who I believe can actually do things on his or her own. Good luck with your job, now go to sleep for God's sake."

I woke up early and went downstairs. There was a banner waiting for me with fourteen unenthused siblings and one over-enthused mother. Besides the banner, there was also a birthday cake. What? Yeah, my mother had absolutely splurged and spent the extra twenty dollars to buy an actual cake. It was quite the indulgence, economically, and calorically. My siblings were pretty unhappy that my mother had only bought a cake for my birthday, the one they all hated.

"Happy birthday!" my mother cheered merrily.

"Thanks, mom. This is really nice of you!" I said sincerely.

"Mom, why didn't we get birthday cakes for our birthdays, but the dingus did?" my fourth brother, Jackson, asked.

"Well, he just started a new job, and we're all feeling down, so a little indulgence will cheer us up!" My mother said hopefully.

"So, basically, you bought the cake because you're feeling depressed and it just happened to be Austin's birthday?" my second brother asked.

"Fine. I was trying to be nice to Austin, but nevermind. I'm just feeling bad and wanted to indulge, I even tried to act nice yesterday. I tried appreciating him, but that failed, and I do not know what to even do with him anymore."

"Great," I said, even though I'd known it was too good to be true.

"Awesome! Let's have some cake!" my younger sister said innocently.

I'm sharing this with you just to show that my family is not only dumb but also to show you what they actually talked about in their free time. Conversation overhead from my bedroom after storming upstairs:

"How do we even eat it?"

"Do we just grab it?"

"Ain't it just a giant cupcake?"

33

"I mean, maybe we slice it."

"From the side?"

"Sure."

"Be careful with that knife, Melissa!"

"Well, I guess this method of eating cake works."

"Dang, I feel rich!"

"Are we sure just grabbing hunks of the cake and slapping them on the plate is the proper way to do it?"

"I betcha twenty bucks it's the way rich people do it."

"You do not have twenty bucks."

"Won't need it, cuz I am right."

"Anywhoo, how's school?"

"Friggin stupid. I do not care about the sixty-seventh element, Dysprosium."

"Sixty-sixth."

"You still buttering up teachers to get better test scores?"

"Either it's working, or my teachers do not know basic addition."

The brisk wind slowed me on my walk to St. Paul. I can not believe I'm going to the capital! It's a long walk. I am going to the wondrously inferior capital city of St. Paul in order to apply for a job at a former library turned museum. Yes, I know I said that it's boring, but I honestly do not

34

care anymore. I'll switch to weekend shifts at the convenience store and work weekdays at the museum. At least I'll get paid a decent amount to work at the boring museum. You know what'd be great? If somehow, in some messed-up way, I got to access the books they have there. I really hope that happens. Oh, how I dream of impossible things.

Man, that walk was long. I passed many convenience stores, medicinal pharmacies, and hotels on my way there. As soon as I crossed city lines, it was pretty clear. Besides the obvious seventeen-foot by seventeen-foot sign welcoming visitors into the capital of Minnesota, there was also a noticeable decrease in the number of buildings and the quality of buildings.

I was psyched to get another job. I had studied all the boring vocabulary words about architecture and literature. Oh my goodness! I could've learned that all in school. I stayed up all last night just reading flashcards, it's like two different languages. Corinthian. Aesopian. Those words do not sound real. If you're reading this in the future, you can not tell me those words sound real. Oh man! If you're reading this in the future, I must sound so weird. The entire English language has probably changed. New-New English. That'd be cool.

I finally got to the building after all that walking, and the building's architecture didn't live up to the hype. I mean, it was just square concrete. What the heck? The book had described decades-old libraries as being all modernist with glass walls and oddly shaped bases and things jutting out for no other reason than fun. This was literally a concrete slab with a hollowed out core. The sign just simply said: *Ancient Library Museum.*

Ancient? Who were they kidding? That exact building was built in 2055 originally as a parking lot for smart cars and was made into a library in 2062. This library was only eight years older than me.

I strode into the building with absolute, unearned confidence. I arrived at the desk and playfully tapped my fingers as I waited. A staff member who looked like she would've rather seen any other human being on this planet or another than me.

"Tour reservation name?" she said in a raspy, irritated voice.

"Actually, I'm coming here for a job interview."

The lady paused and stared me dead in the pupils and looked me up and down and then again as if she were assessing me, and after what felt like ten minutes, she replied, "Congrats, you're a janitor. Uniforms are in the broom closet. We pay ten bucks an hour. You'll work on weekdays after school."

"What sections?" I asked excitedly.

She lowered her glasses and stared for a second, "One-A through Ten-Z."

"Thanks," I said, not knowing how to reply to sarcasm.

I walked into the small broom closet and looked for a uniform. There was one dusty one in the corner with the name "PAT" plastered on it in large, permanent, marker streaks. I didn't want to bother the rude desk worker again, so I dealt with it. There was also a classic yellow mop and water setup. Being a janitor has not changed at all throughout the ages. That's too bad; there's not much to be changed about the job except the pay.

I walked out of the cramped broom closet and wheeled my janitor cart out with me.

"You start next Monday, put that all back," the worker scoffed.

I put the "stuff" back by command and walked all the way back to Eden Prairie. It was another very long walk. I was pretty hungry when I got home, but everyone else had gone to sleep. I grabbed a meal tube and sat down in the language library.

English hasn't changed; it's still such a weird language. I learned about prepositions this time. Also, I got sidetracked and started noticing the differences between some of the English dictionaries. The British one has slang like crisps, the American one has slang I'm used to, like chips, and the Australian one has slang so foreign that it sounds alien, like using chips to describe French fries. Also, certain words are spelled differently than others in the American one, like canceled and *cancelled* or behavior and *behaviour*. Oh well, I should head to bed soon.

Chapter Four

Hello, my name is now Gennadiya. I am an escapee from northern Georgia. It's exhausting keeping up this identity. Especially in prison. Yes, I'm in prison. No, I didn't give in and reveal who I actually am. No, I do not have any of the wonderful and somewhat necessary privileges I could've gotten if I'd revealed myself. Yes, I am bothered by that fact.

On that day, I was charged with murder. I shot Dimos Vassallos at the end of his long, boring, and entirely insane speech. I could've gotten out of it if I revealed who I was, as rulers of any kind (internationally) cannot be arrested under any circumstance. This just goes to show how dedicated I am to escaping. I plan to escape Istanbul and make a new life for myself. A new life, not in any major city or even country, but in some sort of safehaven.

I want to dwell in a place away from society. I want to dwell in a place away from Greek politicians. I want to dwell in a place where I do not receive the royal treatment. I want to dwell in a place where society is actually right, and not corrupt. Most importantly, I want to dwell in a place no one's heard of so that no one can track me down. Until I find that place and go there, I shall be known as Gennadiya Petrov, a Russian refugee from Shovi, Georgia.

I do not know what prison used to be like, but it's certainly worse now. I have found a group of trusted people the week or so I've been here. There are two others about my age who were arrested that night for protesting. We're all in a cell together. Yuce Catli was arrested for attempted assault of an officer. Yeah right, *attempted* assault. I saw her before, I, you know, shot Dimos Vassallos. She totally beat that guy up. Then there's Ali Ertugrul. He was arrested for shooting Qamar Gabris. He was aiming for Dimos but missed. Qamar Gabris and Dimos Vassallos had both been shot within three seconds of each other. Ali was supportive of Qamar Gabris because of his ideocratic beliefs and ideas.

If you saw Ali Ertugrul, you would never think that he *missed* who he was shooting at. He's tall and muscular and was carrying a gun with a license. He is super chagrined that he missed, but he's pretty happy that I didn't. Yuce is also pretty tough. Altogether, in my opinion, we could probably bust out of this prison.

One way we could break out is by negotiating with the guards and luring them to a vulnerable position where one of us can escape as a distraction, and the others actually escape. Meanwhile, the others, who are outside already, help the one being chased escape. The problem with this plan is that there is a ninety percent chance we'll fail entirely.

Plan B would probably be using Yuce's gun. They obviously took the weapons away from me and Ali, because they knew we had them because they saw us shoot major Greek politicians with them. But they forgot to check Yuce. Greeks are inventive and clever, but they can not figure out how to run a prison.

We devised a plan through whispering, and not one guard came to check on us. Tomorrow, at 8:45 AM, when we're transitioning into breakfast, our plan will start. We have figured out that we are guarded by the least people at that time. We just have to shoot two people and then run away. It's not that hard. I've had more trouble learning Italian history and not laughing.

We have spent hours designing our plan. We know all the exits and we are absolutely ready. I, of course, have the best aim and will be shooting the gun. It's as simple as "*BANG! BANG! RUN!*" But if it's that simple, then why am I so incredibly worried?

It's 8:30 and we are right on schedule. Yuce's gun is loaded and I have it hidden in my jacket pocket. Ali is totally ready to punch a guy in the face if he needs to; he always is. Suddenly, for the first time in my history here at this humble Greek prison in Turkey, a guard came to check on us.

"Come on out. Do not be afraid. We're leaving early for a speech," the officer said in a gruff and groggy voice.

"Wha-?" I started to ask.

"Do not ask questions," he interrupted.

I looked to Ali and Yuce for help or an explanation, but they were even more confused than I was. We were led down a long set of corridors with the rest of the people in the section. There were somehow twice as many guards as prisoners in that line. It seemed as though the Greeks had upped their security. We walked throughout the entirety of the prison, only to end up in the rarely-used and consequently rarely-cleaned mess hall.

Standing at the podium was Antonis Melis, the military director who I mentioned before. He was an ideocratic general who directed the majority of the Greek military and he was the one in the tank that killed my father. Although he shared Qamar's ideocratic ideology, he did not agree with Qamar's individual type of abstract thinking.

I did not explain what ideocracy is. Ideocracy is a form of social construct or government that is based on one's individualized abstract thinking. If a government is ideocratic, the ruler or rulers base the government off of their abstract thinking, meaning that while it is relative to the country's issues, it is resolved using international or regional solutions. They look at the broader picture, rather than looking at the specific problem. For instance, if Greece had a lead contamination water crisis, they would hold a regional conference to work with countries near the Bosphorus and the Black Sea on how to better improve water quality as a whole in the region. There is also a type of abstract thinking in which one will think outside of reality in order to find a solution. In this type of abstract thinking, one would announce to Greece that they had upset the environment and gradually fix the problem in a controlled area. In Greek political vocabulary, the former one of the types is known as Qamaranism, whilst the latter is known as Antonianism. You can probably guess which politicians the ideologies got their names from.

Ideocracy is never to be confused with ideocracy. Ideocracy is an act or action that arises from an idea or belief that is rather idiotic. I apologize if I do ever misuse that vocabulary. Back on the subject of ideocracy, Greek politicians are now mostly Qamarinist or Antonianist. Nikolas Dellis is absolutely Qamaranist. Thalis Pappas is somewhat Antonianist, although he believes people should be realistic in all circumstances. Trifonas Ballas is Qamaraist and has convinced the majority of the Greek population to be Qamaranist as well. Finally, Minas Mattas is Antonianist. As you can see, the playing field of Greek politics seems to be almost balanced between Qamaranism and Antonianism.

Antonis Melis was at the podium, waiting for everyone to be silenced and seated. He waited for a long time. There were hundreds of prisoners cooped up in that malodorous mess hall. No one was expecting this, especially not me, but I still had my gun.

He cleared his throat excessively and then started talking with a heavy Greek accent "Hello." The crowd already seemed to hate the air he breathed. "I am Antonis Melis, a Greek military director. I am coming here today, and to all other prisons in the empire to make an announcement that was made yesterday. First off, happy new year, it is officially 2092," the prisoners grumbled, "Secondly, I would like to announce that the Neo-Ottoman Empire has been divided. All land west of Istanbul in the former empire is now part of the Greek Empire. All land east in the empire is now part of the Arabic State." The prisoners started to get angry as he continued,

"The Arabic State will be a puppeted region of the Greek Empire with semi-independence. By semi-independence, I mean that the Arabic state shall have a sultan, yet he or she will be overseen by the New Greek government. An election will be held in a month over who will be the sultan of the Arabic State, but until then, the Arabic State will be entirely under the control of the Greek government." The prisoners started shouting at him and booing. "The Greek Empire shall be ruled by a co-parliamentary system. One Qamaranist representative and one Antonianist representative shall vote on all issues involving the Greek government, with a third representative of neither ideology as the tie-breaker. All issues involving the Arabic State shall be decided by a vote as well, however, the sultan will have one vote, whilst the other representatives and the tie-breaker shall have two votes. Thank you for your time." Antonis walked off stage.

The prisoners were certainly not enraged by his speech. It was very different from hearing Dimos's speech in the town center. After Dimos's speech, the crowds protested actively. But in prison, protesting was absolutely not an option. After the speech, ended, we went to the meal hall and I sat down with Yuce and Ali. We were served the usual, oatmeal goop breakfast tubes. The three of us immediately started talking about the speech.

"Well, that was quite the speech," Yuce stated.

"I can not believe that Antonis Melis was next in command," the Qamaranist Ali said.

"I just can not believe that he divided the entire Neo-Ottoman State. He even said explicitly that the Arabic State's sultan would have one less vote than the Qamaranist Greek representative, the Antonianist Greek representative, and the Greek tie-breaker. That's simply unjust, we gave them more representation when ruling over them!" I chimed in.

"Calm down, I mean, they conquered the entirety of the strongest empire on Earth in less than two hours, I think they deserve credit. It was pretty stupid to not have people guarding the sultan and the heir. Also, the heir could've warned the sultan through a telegram."

"It took them forty-five years. The least we could've done is given their military a decent shot."

"Yeah, but it's odd how fast they killed the heir. Wasn't the actual battle literally right in front of the heir's house?"

"That's right, Yuce. The battle played out entirely in front of the heir's house. They had a million chances to escape, and now they're dead and there was no one to rule the Neo-Ottoman Empire."

"Maybe they were just overconfident in the Ottoman military, maybe they thought the Neo-Ottoman Empire would win the battle, which makes sense considering that throughout every battle held in front of the Bosphorus, the Neo-Ottoman Empire has always won," I said, desperately trying to defend myself and not let them know who I really was.

"While then they were stupid. No matter what, you always have to be prepared for war."

I stayed quiet for the rest of breakfast, as I was quite chagrined about what Ali and Yuce had said about me, even though I know they didn't mean it, as they do not know who I am. I went back to our cell and started reading a book. It was a language comprehension guide. It was not a dictionary, but a book that specifically taught you the language.

I was learning German, as I was considering Berlin as a safehaven. It was entirely destroyed in the nuclear fallout of 2027 and unlike some of the other cities, it hadn't been rebuilt after it. No one lives in Berlin, and the closest airport is two-hundred-fifty miles away. You would be crazy to live in Berlin. There is not a single building that wasn't destroyed, and there are remnants of the DC Virus there. I didn't want to be like people in the Americas or Asia, who were always sick. It must be so expensive to constantly buy new medicine each month. If I lived in Berlin, and I got infected by the DC Virus, I would have to go all the way out to Hamburg or maybe Minsk just to get medicine. That would be really expensive, but it'd be absolutely worth it. I can not wait to find the perfect safehaven.

I speak five languages, and if I succeed in learning German, six. I speak Turkish, Greek, English, Hindi Turkish, and Bosnian. I speak Turkish as my first language, as I've grown up and lived in Istanbul my entire life. I speak Greek because I need to understand Greek politics, and I live rather near the old Greek border, so many people speak Greek. I learned English because it is almost a universal language now. It is common for people all over the world to learn English because America was once the economic center of the world. Also, it has become one of the go-to languages for schools to teach. I learned English in school. I might explain how that all works later. I had to learn Hindi Turkish for the time when my father and I went to India on a political trip not so long ago in 2089 after we fully regained control of the Indian subcontinental area. I speak Bosnian because I had to go on many political trips throughout Bosnia because the Neo-Ottoman Empire constantly needed to support the Bosnian governments.

After about an hour or two of learning German, I got bored. I decided to see if Ali or Yuce knew any games. By the way, no one had said anything about how our plan had failed.

"Ali, do you know of any games we could play? I am pretty bored." I asked.

"Yeah, you have to expect that when you're literally in the most boring place describable on Earth, prison," Ali replied.

"I have a game I smuggled in that I got from a vacation in America when I was seven," Yuce said.

"Must be vintage" I stupidly commented.

"It's a game called Mo-No-Po-Ly. Even when I got it, it was considered an insanely old game. I found it in a cute, little, antique shop labeled as a Capitalist Propaganda game."

"Sounds interesting, but slightly illegal. Let's do it. It's better than waiting around while absolutely nothing happens."

Yuce pulled out the game and started setting up, "I feel like a kid in the early 2000s playing a board game for no reason other than fun."

There were tons of little pieces and doohickeys. There was a bunch of fake cash and some not-so-well written instructions. They were in English, Spanish, and French. We could all understand them. All of us know how to speak English. It took a good, long while for us to set up the game, but it took even longer to play it. Did kids in the early 2000s have nine hours to play a single, boring game? Also, the game was VERY capitalist. It was quite the American game, you bought properties, you went to jail a lot, and you paid an excessive amount of money in taxes that other random players will get based on what space they land on. Sounds like America to me. My question is: was it Pro-Capitalist propaganda or Anti-Capitalist propaganda? If it was Anti-Capitalist, then it definitely did a good job. If I ever end up in a throne, I will make sure not to establish a capitalist government. If it was Pro-Capitalist, then what the heck were they thinking when they made that game? No matter what, how was a piece of propaganda a popular American board game?

We still had not discussed any future plans for breaking out. I still had my, I mean Yuce's, gun. Maybe I could do this on my own. However, I was getting accustomed to how accommodating prison cells were after the newly instated Greek regulations of prison quality. We had a tan (or maybe beige?) shag carpet that was easily stained. We had a plethora of games and books in that cell. Although they were of an understandably, cruddy quality, it was much, much better than having no distractions. Besides the many books we have in our cells, which is about three or so assorted books, there is a small library by the mess hall we are allowed to visit if we ask a guard. In our cell, we have an English dictionary, a Gaelic Encyclopedia (who even speaks Gaelic anymore?), and an Italian romance novel. I had heard of the library via Berke Ozker, an acquaintance I met in prison who's been here for a long while. I was very excited to see if they had a German dictionary.

An officer walked by my cell, and I tried to catch his attention, "Excuse me, officer? May I visit the library?" Wow, I really sound like a Georgian refugee peasant. I'm almost ashamed of how I act.

The officer grunted and let me out of the cell. "Half-an-hour, you'll be guarded all the way through the time because of the severity of your crime."

"Thank you very, very, very much, sir." In the name of Gok Tengri, I wish I didn't have to act so poorly. Why did I use so many very's? What was I thinking? Someone was going to catch on.

The officer grunted and pulled me out of the cell. Ali asked if he could come, and the officer said yes. However, we now need one point five times more officers. Ali didn't say why he wanted to go to the library. I thought that he might want to check out a dictionary. The walk to the library wasn't that long. It was much closer than the mess hall. There were myriad officers following us, which made Ali and me incredibly nervous. I forgot to put my gun away! I realized that fact much too late. I would get in some serious trouble if they found it. I would be put in solitary! I had to make sure they did not find out, or, maybe, I could shoot forty-five officers with one gun and no backup. That was unlikely to happen.

I just hoped that they didn't find my gun. I held the right flap of my jacket over on the left, so it covered up the lump made by Yuce's gun. One officer looked over, and it seemed like he saw my gun. He pulled aside another officer and pointed at where my "gun lump" was. I tensed up and dropped my, I mean, Yuce's gun, luckily, I caught it with my pocket. I was tenser than I had ever been in my life. I held in my stomach and sucked my gut in. I pretended to look away, despite both officers literally staring me down. Although it was only about four or five seconds, it felt like a million years. The officer waved the other off, and we continued on our way to the library. Ali looked down at me and made sure I knew to be careful. I should not have asked to go to the library. This was quite a dumb idea.

If I went to the library and I was caught, I would get put in solitary. But, at the library, I could find very important resources, such as German dictionaries.

"Here we are, we'll follow you throughout the library. Do not try to pull any crap or somethin' on us." the leading officer said.

"Okay, sir. May you show me where the dictionaries are located in the library?" I asked.

The guard pointed haphazardly down a corridor filled with dictionaries. The officer, as he said he would, followed me down the aisle. I stopped at the European languages section. It was organized alphabetically by language. I scanned past Bulgarian, Czech, Danish, English, French, Gaelic, and then found German. The German dictionary was quite beat up. I took it and looked around. I wondered if there were any Turkish dictionaries or dictionaries based on languages that are denominations of the Turkish language. I scanned my eyes past the many alphabetical sections after German and ended up with nothing. I looked more carefully this time, from each dictionary to the next. There wasn't a Turkish dictionary, let alone a Turkish denomination dictionary. I looked up to the guard, confused.

"Why aren't there any Turkish dictionaries here?" I asked as if the guard had the answer.

"They removed them in an attempt to stop people from learning about Turkish history and getting involved in politics, the government believes that the fewer people know about the past, the less they will care about the future, and that includes politics." He explained.

It seemed that he did, in fact, know, "What about actual Turkish history books? Surely they can not remove that many books."

The guard chuckled, "Oh, yes, they did. Look over to the left and down two aisles, you'll see."

I followed his instructions and came face to face with a wall of books that had been removed, "Where did they all go? That's insane for them to think we'll just forget about Turkish history!"

"Well, how do you know so much about Turkish history, if you're from Georgia?" the guard asked inquisitively.

"Well, I mean- I, I- y, know. I guess I just have an interest in history." I shrugged.

"Who won the Battle of Sakhoista?"

"What?"

"You heard me."

"The Ottoman Empire, like they always do." I couldn't believe I said something so pro-Ottoman. He would definitely smell a rat.

"Well then, you know your history," he laughed, but then immediately asked, "Who won the Battle of Hue in Vietnam?"

"The US and South Vietnamese forces," I responded instantly. I know my bloody history.

"Who won the Battle of Mexico City, in 2083?"

"American forces," I said, feeling rather smart.

"Well, you do know your history," he chuckled. It seems as if I had gotten on the guard's good side.

"My name is Gennadiya. It's nice to meet you." I stuck out my hand for a handshake.

"My name is Shegan, and the pleasure is mine. I'm sorry you have to be in this place. I know what you did, and to be entirely and completely honest, I agree with what you did."

"Wow, that's quite the statement for a GREEK prison guard to state," I said awkwardly.

"Well, I'm from Albania. I've never agreed with Greek politics, but I've had to tolerate them through my life."

I turned around and saw an odd and circular device. "What is that?" I pointed to the unidentified object like a peasant girl with absolutely no manners whatsoever.

"That, if I am not mistaken, is a record player."

"Well, I got the book I needed, why do not you explain to me how it's used?"

"It's not what you think. It's not a security device or anything. It's a recreational device."

"What?"

"Here, you just place a record on it," he said as he placed a very large, thin, circular disk onto it, "and you place the needle on the record like so." Oddly loud music started to fill the room.

"What song is this?"

"It's, um, some dumb American thing."

"Well, luckily, I speak English."

How many roads must a man walk down..... Before you can call him a man?

"That question seems subjective. If I was a boy and spent four years of my life walking down hundreds of roads and nothing else, I wouldn't be considered mature enough to be a man, or would I? This song is confusing."

How many seas must a white dove sail…. Before she sleeps in the sand?

"What is a white dove? I think it's a bird. But why would a bird be in the sand, sleeping nonetheless?"

"Well, a white dove used to be a symbol of peace that was to come, so when it had time to rest in the sand, peace would have been achieved."

"I do not think a simple song can have that much meaning."

Yes, 'n' how many times must the cannonballs fly.. Before they're forever banned?

"I kind of get that one. This music is making me think too hard. That was a dumb idea."

Shegan stopped the record and turned back towards me, "Well, it's about time to leave anyway."

"Oh well. That was quite fun. You've made prison more fun that I thought it could be."

"Well thank you. And hey, tomorrow, I'll put your cell on laundry machine cleaning out duty. It's the simplest job. All you do is take the tons of coins that have been dumped in there and put them back in the basket so we can continue to use the machines."

"Thank you very much."

53

"By the way," Shegan hesitated and looked down while biting on his lip, but then looked back up. "I know about the gun."

Chapter Five

Mopping the floor sounds like a very monotonous and boring task, and it very much is. But hey, I'm getting paid a reasonably decent amount. However, on the bright side, I do have access to the actual library, as I need to clean it. If I cleaned all the sections very quickly, I could probably nab some time to look at an atlas. My plan was starting to fold out in front of me. I only came here after school, so all of the tours were done or very close to wrapping up. I go in and I have three and a half hours to clean the entire building. It may seem like a small amount of time, and it may seem like a large amount of time, but I think it's way too much time to clean one building. That just means that I'll indisputably have extra time, where no one will bother me, and I can find a safehaven in an atlas. I doubt there will be any updated atlases, so I'll just need to guess and hope the country hasn't been recolonized or something or other.

I just realized I have never really talked about school. The school I go to is near the city but is actually on the border exactly in order to save money on taxes. All the rich kids from Minneapolis and St. Paul go there, and all of the regular people everywhere else near the Minneapolis-St. Paul region. There is quite a division between those who can afford a car and gas every day and those who can not, to put it in simpler terms. It's a large and fairly modern looking building. There are three floors, one is a Hmong floor, and the other is an English floor, and the base floor is a German floor. As you can tell, the classes are separated by language. For learning other languages, we are just sent to the Language and Literature class on another floor, so it's in another language. I am currently learning English as my secondary, and German a Hmong where I take my primary classes, such as regular Language and Literature or Maths.

I suppose I should talk about my life at school. At school, like at my house, I can constantly go unnoticed, which means I can occasionally not abide by the rules, and I am very unpopular. It's bad enough that my family hates me, but everyone at school hates me too. Maybe I just have an extremely toxic personality. Maybe it's the fact that I barely ever talk to people.

That's enough talk about my miserably miserable life at school. I'd rather talk about what happened on the third day of my job. The first two days of my job were fabulously dull and tedious. My third day was interesting, to say the least. I finished two hours earlier than I was supposed to, and it made sense. I barely cleaned the floor, I swept over briskly and ran through the building doing that. I finished in one and one-half hours, meaning that I took my sweet time briskly sweeping over the floor. If I didn't get fired for the quality of the job that I did that day, or thereof lack of, then that would show what kind of business was being run at this fatefully old museum that provided tours for those who wanted to learn about one of the most boring subjects I could even think about: libraries.

In the two hours I had left, I rushed through the library; looking for an atlas. First I looked in the geography section, but it was the only history there, I had to double-check and triple-check because that was bogus. Then,

I looked in history, where there were only geography books, which was also bogus, meaning I had to double check every book in the section again and twice more again. I had given up. It was clear someone had rearranged the entire library, switching many sections with many others. As I was on my way out, an hour and seventeen minutes early, I saw an atlas next to the dictionary. Those two books were in plastic cases on podiums near the entrance, they were the most commonly asked about books, so they were near the entrance so visitors wouldn't have to ask.

Was I desperate enough to break those cases simply to get access to an atlas? Heck yes, I would. I braced my fist for the impact with the hard plastic, and yet I could never brace myself enough for the pain. In the name of the ancient Hmong settlers in Thailand kept in camps, why did it have to hurt so much if it was just plastic? I took a minute or two recovering from the pain of the blow. I was quite excited to see the atlas, so I didn't wait that long. My hand was still slightly bleeding as I reached down into that wretched case to get the atlas. And then, papercut. As my hand bled, my papercut added to the pain.

I reached for the atlas and tore it from its chamber. The atlas was no longer trapped in the enclosure that had held it for decades. If only the atlas could talk, it would be shouting, for it was finally free! Jeez, I was acting so happy for the darn atlas, probably because I will still in extreme shock from the friggin' pain. Jesus Christ!! I couldn't feel a single part of my body. Why did I do this? I was having a stage nine meltdown in the middle of a library less than two and a half hours before I needed to get home, and oh, boy, everything hurt! So there I was, rolling around on the floor in the middle of a library just because I wanted an atlas. I had done this to myself. Oh my goodness, you would probably believe this was the first time I experienced any pain in my life, but it was not at all!

After my wondrously over-reactive meltdown, I opened the atlas. Alas, nothing really popped out at me. At first, there was a bunch of copyright crap, and then there were climate maps of the world, and the transportation maps, then population maps, then time zone maps, then finally, there was a world political map. In the upper left, there was North America. Wow! This atlas was super-duper old! It must have been made in 2018 or something! North America was still at peace at that time. This was before the literal nuclear fallout happened. The city of Angelo was labeled as Los Angeles on the map, which was fun to see. There used to be so many tiny countries in Central America, of course, that was before the major political fallout of 2072. Woah! There were many islands in the Caribbean before the US got worried about communism in the west (yet again) and nuked and invaded the living daylights out of the tiny Caribbean countries. This was even before the nuclear fallout. Greenland was a part of Denmark, apparently. Surprisingly, not much has changed in South America, most of the original borders have been restored since the political fallout. Africa! Oh boy, it has changed excessively! There isn't even a single country in Africa in 2092! Wow! There were so many countries in Africa in 2018! Europe has changed a lot. There are so many empires nowadays. This empire owns this country and whatnot. Turkey was very small before the assassination of

Erdogan. Russia! That used to exist, I guess! It used to be really big, almost as large as the Neo-Ottoman Empire is now! Kazakhstan? Nepal? Bhutan? Indonesia? I've never heard of these places. Bhutan, Nepal, and Bangladesh are now all part of the Indian Territory under the Neo-Ottoman Empire. Speaking of the Neo-Ottoman Empire, there's something or other going down right now. Someone died or something. I do not pay much attention to what the newspapers say. I knew that the Taiwanese Dynasty controls all of Russia, Mongolia, China, Japan, Taiwan, the Philippines, some regions in Southeast Asia, and some regions above some of the *stans*. What's Sri Lanka? I wonder if they're part of the Indian territories.

Then, I looked at the bottom right. That was where I didn't know anything about the countries. Yes! I had found a potential region for a safehaven. Not only is it super far from the rest of the functioning society, but no one's heard of the places there! Also, I would've read about any history that happened in this Oceanic region, and I remember nothing about this region ever happening, meaning that all of the places have probably stayed untouched by the rest of society, and they haven't been colonized or anything like that!

I frantically looked in the Oceanic region, hoping to see an interesting name. Australia? No, they had too much history before the fallouts, they're probably too developed. New Zealand? Same problem. Papua New Guinea? No, that name stressed me out. I looked closely at the ocean, and would you believe it, there were countries there! New Caledonia? No, they used to be owned by France colonially. Too developed.

I looked through the ocean, hoping something would catch my eye. Fiji? No, cannibalism is legal there. Turns out that Oceania did have a lot of history. A lot. Nauru? Went bankrupt, the population moved away, meaning there are no airports. The Solomon Islands? Volcanic. Niue?

Maybe Niue would work. Maybe Niue is the safehaven! Wait, I think I remember something about that country. The government turned into a very weird cult. Also, all of the airports were shut down after runway troubles came about. Nevermind about Niue being a safehaven.

Tuvalu? Wasn't that one of the countries that almost sank? Yeah, that and the Maldives. Luckily, the UN gave funds to Tuvalu to build artificial islands. Stupid UN! So that's it. Tuvalu is the safehaven. Next time, I will go to the history section and find the history of Tuvalu to double-check that it's not such a bad place.

It was three days since I had "discovered" Tuvalu. What a place! I now know every single thing there is to know about Tuvalu. I had asked my teacher in Social Studies, and she said she didn't know what I was talking about! Yes! Victory! No one knew about it! I have done such an extensive amount of research about the wondrous country of Tuvalu that I now probably know more about Tuvalu than anyone else! I found a lot of books, and I tore out a couple of very important pages for later. Here is a quote from a history book I found:

"Tuvalu is a modern-day commonwealth country consisting of 124 islands and islets, there are 9 main islands, represented by the 9 stars on the flag. Tuvalu means "8 Standing Together" in Tuvaluan since there were only 8 inhabited islands when it was discovered.

Polynesian migration to Tuvalu began about 3,000 years ago from Samoa. When discovered by the Samoans, it was incorporated into the Tu'i Manu'a Confederacy. Later, after the decline of Tu'i Manu'a in the 11th century, Tongans put Tuvalu into their sphere of influence. Four times in the 15th and 16th century, the Tu'i Tonga Empire invaded Tuvalu, two times in Niutao. Then, in the 17th century, Gilbertese warriors from Kiribati invaded two times and failed.

The first European contact with Tuvalu was by Álvaro de Mendaña de Neira in 1568 in a Spanish expedition. Álvaro de Mendaña de Neira passed by the southernmost Tuvaluan island in 1595. In 1764, John Byron charted the islands as the Lagoon Islands. In 1819, British explorers passed by Tuvalu. European whalers started whaling in Tuvalu in 1821. Christianity was introduced in 1861 by a Christian Deacon from the Cook Islands. Trading in Tuvalu began in Funafuti in the 1850s.

In 1876, Germany and Britain decided to split up the western and central Pacific into spheres of influence. In 1877, the governor of Fiji was given the sphere of influence that included Tuvalu and Kiribati. Starting in 1892, Tuvalu was a British protectorate. In 1916, the administration of the Gilbert and Ellice Islands was established. The United States landed in

Tuvalu in 1942 Ellice to prepare for an oncoming invasion from nearby Japanese-owned Kiribati. Many airfields and air bases were built. Many important battles in the War happened in Kiribati, with the American troops coming from Tuvalu. By 1945, the Pacific War had ended and all troops had been deployed elsewhere, one of the leftover military bases was developed into the Funafuti International Airport, which is currently the only airport in Tuvalu.

After the separation of the Administration of the Gilbert and Ellice Islands, Britain gradually transitioned Tuvalu and Kiribati into self-governance. Tuvalu officially gained independence in 1978."

That was a very useful book! It told me everything I needed to know about Tuvalu! Wow! Now all I have to do is wait a year or so to save up enough money! Okay, writing that makes me realize I could probably just steal money from my parents or others in order to get out of here faster. I mean, if I got arrested, life would still be better than mine is now.

I still work shifts at the convenience store. I could casually steal all of the money in the register for a few days, and no one would notice. But, on the third or fourth weekend, someone would smell a rat. Either because the building the convenience store is in is absolutely infested in rats, but also because it's unusual to not have any customers for that amount of time for so many days. For one to two weekends it's entirely regular to have no customers in the afternoon.

On the weekends, using USD to estimate, the store racks in about eighty to one hundred dollars on a busy day, and twenty to sixty dollars on a regular day. If I took half of the money each day, which would average to sixty-five dollars, give or take twenty dollars. On one weekend, I could make up to one-hundred-forty dollars extra on the weekend. On top of that, I am paid seven dollars and sixty cents an hour on the weekend shifts. I work six hours on the weekends now, meaning I get ninety-one dollars and twenty cents on one weekend. Together, that's about two-hundred-thirty dollars, give or take ten dollars or so.

On the weekdays, I am paid ten dollars an hour for three and a half hours. That is thirty-five dollars per day. Over one week (excluding the weekend), I make one-hundred-seventy-five dollars at the museum. Together with the weekend shifts and the stealing, that would be around four-hundred and five dollars in one week! Wow! Stuff can add up! Unsurprisingly, the highest money-maker is the stealing from the cash register.

According to my calculations, which took me a while, I could make enough money for the flight to Tuvalu in less than eight weeks! That is considering that a flight of that length at lowest class could cost thirty-two-hundred dollars, give or take about fifty-four bucks. That is also considering a fixed rate. That is also considering that my math was a very rough estimation. That is also considering anyone even still lives there.

Yikes. I sure hope this ends up working.

63

It is the first weekend of my stealing operation. Operation Tuvalu as I like to call it. It had been an okay Saturday so far. We had one leftover meal tube at breakfast and no one but me was hungry. Many customers have come and gone, we have made twenty-nine dollars. I am three hours into my shift. Six customers have come so far. Everything looks on track to be an okay day for sales, except for the fact that I will be taking most of them.

At every transaction with a customer, I leave the register open even after I put their payments in. Then, once they leave, I nab some money out of the drawer and stash it in my pocket whilst no one is looking. I've only done it for five customers, as the last one paid with a coupon.

It has been an hour and a half since I last jotted down an update. Operation Tuvalu is still happening! Four and a half hours into my shift, and ten customers have come, including the ones from the last update. I have continued to sneak money out of the register with no one in the store noticing!

Two people so far have used forms of payment other than cash. One with a coupon, and one with a card. The store has made forty-two dollars four and a half hours in, and I have stolen thirty of those dollars. I am hoping no more people pay in cards or coupons, as that is a circumstance I did not work in the calculations at all, and it could lose me lots of money!

By the way, 30 dollars of forty-two is seventy-one percent. Maybe I have been taking too much at each transaction. I will try from now on to take much less from each transaction.

It has been one-half hour since I last wrote. Only one more customer came, and they paid using their card. That may not seem like a good thing, but their purchase was twenty-five dollars! That means that the percentage of the money I've stolen is much, much less!

This means that I've only stolen less than forty-five percent! Nevermind about taking less at each transaction! By the way, who buys twenty-five dollars worth of crap from a convenience store?

It has been forty-five minutes. I do not expect anyone to come in the next fifteen minutes. Two more customers. Neither paid in card or coupon! Hurrah! Today, in total the five hours and forty-five minutes I've been here, the store has made seventy-one dollars and thirty cents!

Meanwhile, I have made thirty-nine dollars off of this wondrously busy day. I didn't know we could have so many sales in one day! Also, I have only taken about fifty-five percent of the total revenue. That may seem like a large amount, but it's better than taking seventy-one percent of the total revenue. One second, someone's coming into the store.

Twelve people just came in. They were a family. Why does this matter? Because they bought eighty-four dollars worth of supplies. We had never been a convenience store where families get their supplies from. We are much too expensive for that, so most people go to the one across the street when it comes to supplies. The store has made more money than they ever have before! Today, including what I stole so far, the store has made one-hundred and fifty-five dollars and thirty cents! Yes, of course, I stole from them after the family left.

I have taken fifty-five dollars of the one-hundred-fifty-five dollars the store made today. That is less than thirty-six percent of their total revenue. Plus, the manager won't believe me when I tell him how much we made today (excluding what I took)!

Chapter Six

Laundry Duty was not that bad. We had to pick out all of the coins from the laundromat laundry machines and put them back in the coin basket so people could pay for laundry when doing laundry. It happened every six or so months, this time, my cell and those cells adjacent to us had been picked randomly to do the task. I wonder why we were picked.

Although the task sounds boring, it was better than cleaning the gym or cleaning the mess hall. We were told that we could keep at the maximum three coins that we found very interesting. But, once we got out of prison, we had to give it away and back to an officer.

I had one Neo-Soviet coin, one Bermudan coin that was triangular, and I was looking for a third interesting one. I picked the Neo-Soviet coin because it was one of the only coins ever to be colored. It was colored red and had a yellow Communist insignia in the center. I picked the Bermudan coin because it was triangular. I was hoping to find a coin for a safehaven. Bermuda could possibly be a safehaven, if it wasn't colonized, I had to check a history book or something. Again, I should've paid more attention in school when I had the chance.

Then came a German two Reichsmark coin, which was somewhat interesting, considering it was from the Nazi era. I considered taking it, but Germany's history wasn't that unique compared to other countries. Plus, it wasn't oddly-shaped or colored. Then came an American quarter from 2023.

Nothing special. I had seen fifty of those so far, and it had only been an hour.

Ali had found an original Soviet coin! We compared notes and I think I might give him my Neo-Soviet coin so he can have both eras of coins. Yuce found a one pound British coin. Yuce also found a coin from Uzbekistan, which looked similar to an American quarter. But, in between the three of us, we had over one-hundred-eighty assorted lira coins.

We had not found a single Greek coin. When I asked a guard, they responded by telling me that it was "disrespectful to degrade the quality and integrity of a Greek-made object for the use of unnecessary deposits." So, I mean, they banned Turkish books because they were offensive to the Greek government and Greek coins in laundry machines because they were offensive to use for a transaction instead of other types of cash.

An hour of sorting coins has a mental and physical toll on people. My arm has grown tired of the repetitive motion of picking up a coin, holding it closer so I can inspect it, and then dumping it in the basket. Although literally every coin you will ever come across will be lightweight, but after a while, each coin seems to be heavier than the last coin.

Everyone in the room was exhausted and wanted to stop, and we were only one hour into our shift. People were begging guards to let them stop. One person, in particular, had even offered every coin in the room to be given to him if we could leave early. Maybe I was wrong, or dare I say, presumptuous, to state that taking out old coins from old laundry machines would be the most fun, easy, and generally overall enjoyable task of the available tasks?

Maybe the guard had realized that I was so smart and enjoyable to be with, and just decided to give me the worst of all of the jobs. What made him think that the coin-sorting task at the laundromat would be easier than cleaning the gym or the mess hall? Maybe he saw my gun and wanted to make me suffer for as long as I am in this prison before Shegan tattles on me for having a gun that did not even originally belong to me.

Shegan reacted to the gun poorly. He asked how I got it. As I told him more about my fake story (the story of Gennadiya Petrov from Shovi, Georgia), he asked more and more personal questions. After a while, I realized he had been trying to interrogate me. He asked me where and when I was born, who my siblings were, who my parents were, what school I went to, and even how I ended up as a Georgian refugee in a Greek prison in the middle of Turkey.

The question he asked at the end made me think. He asked why I shot Dimos after his speech. That is a good question. Why would a perfectly smart and well-mannered girl who escaped from horrible living conditions in Georgia shoot a major Greek politician after finding out that he was the new ruler of the wondrous Neo-Ottoman State? Why, Gennadiya? Why would you do this? When he asked me, I blanked. I said that I did it because I was hoping to hop on stage and proclaim myself the new ruler of the Neo-Ottoman Empire. Wow! Gennadiya Petrov may know everything about history, but she still sounds like a complete nincompoop!

69

Yes. It definitely would've entirely made sense if, after I shot the ruler of a country after his speech, I could go up and proclaim the throne. Why, of all excuses I could've thought of at that moment (like, I wanted to go down in the history books as someone great), did I have to choose the absolute worst excuse that could ever be used in my current situation? All of the guards found out about this and I am now apparently the biggest idiot in this entire Greek prison.

I was still coin-sorting, and I came across one very peculiar coin. It was circular. On the back side of the coin, it had a picture of Queen Elizabeth the Second with a rather disdainful frown. Around the picture of the queen were the words: *2017 TUVALU 2 DOLLARS QUEEN ELIZABETH II 2OZ 9999 SILVER.* That was a very confusing set of words. What did nine-nine-nine-nine mean? I would bet you the coin weighed two Oz, so that made sense. Tuvalu? What was that? Maybe a country? This coin was pretty old. If Tuvalu was ever a country, it would probably be gone by this point in time. I flipped the coin around and was taken aback. On the obverse side, there was an odd-looking fellow in a futuristic uniform with a mustache and a very, very wrinkled forehead. In the background, there were symbols and nonsensical lines. I couldn't understand the language the symbols were written in. Then, off-center to the center by a strand of hair, there was a logo saying: *STAR TREK THE NEXT GENERATION 30.* Perhaps Star Trek was a show, the next generation was an episode, and 30 was the episode number assigned to that episode?

I got up from my very busy workstation and walked over to one of the guards (NOT SHEGAN).

I tapped him politely on the shoulder, "Excuse me, sir? I believe that this coin is a counterfeit."

The guard was baffled, "Why would someone ever use a counterfeit coin? How would someone even get one into this prison? I can guarantee that it's probably not counterfeit."

"Well sir, the back looks like it could possibly be a real coin, but the back is covered in symbols that make absolutely zero sense!"

The guard laughed, "Oh! I've heard of these. Many, many decades ago, the Perth Mint, that's the place in Perth where they used to make coins, decided to make coins for this little, insignificant country in the Pacific known as *Tu-Vahhh-Loo,* and they, together, the two governments thought they could both drawn in revenue if they made pop-culture coins that weren't to be used, but collected. And so they did. The coins were astonishingly rare, and so the prices went through the roof! I think this tiny coin alone was worth over eight-hundred-fifteen liras! People went crazy for these little coins even though you couldn't pay for them! They had made coins for all sorts of crazy pop-culture crap!"

"Wow. That is a pretty weird story. I think that'll be one of the coins I keep, because of such the interesting story. How did you know that, if you do not mind me asking?"

"Well, I grew up an Aussie. I loved nothing more than those quirky coins, and one day, I quit my job and decided to start working there. It was very fun! It may seem like a boring job to you, but it was fun to do little work for a large pay! Anyway, I should probably tell you to get back to your work over there with the coins and the laundry machine and the coin basket."

I walked away, smiling from the nice interaction.

"Hey!" I turned around. "Niue had a similar licensing deal."

Tuvalu. *TooVallOooh*. Weird name. So is Niue. *Nooheyy*. I decided to do a bit of research in the library. I avoided Shegan excessively. I went into the library yet again. I went past the empty Turkish history section, and into the rest of the history section. It was arranged by continent and alphabetically. What continent were these countries in? Niue sounds like an Asian country. Tuvalu sounds like a fake country, but if I had to guess a continent Tuvalu is in, I would guess South America. But wait, I thought! The licensing deal involved Perth. Perth is in Australia! So, I thought that Tuvalu and Niue either had to be in Southeast Asia or Australia (otherwise known as Oceania for you Spaniards), so I looked in those sections.

The continent of Australia was put under the name of Oceania. Oh well, I was in a somewhat European place. Asia was split into subcontinents. Western Asia, Eastern Asia, the Middle East, the Indian Subcontinent, and Southeast Asia. I looked through Southeast Asia. Nothing. They still had Burma instead of Myanmar. Interesting. Very interesting. Then, I looked in Oceania. Oceania was a very odd and unique part of the world. I do not know of anything that has happened in that entire continent since the Oceanic Growth Period in 2066.

Australia was the first. I looked down through the books. Of all of the continent sections, Oceania had the least books. Niue was next to New Zealand. I nabbed the book, hoping to find the perfect safehaven. Hoping to find a new life. And then I looked in the book and the first thing it said was: "Niue is a territory of New Zealand." I closed the book.

New Zealand was NOT a safehaven. That also means that Niue is NOT a safehaven. New Zealand is the most developed part of Oceania. Australia was the second most developed. They were the only countries that actually developed during the Oceanic Growth Period. No one else has even heard of any of the other countries in Oceania.

I practically tossed that dumb future-spoiling book back on that dumb future-spoiling shelf. I looked back down on the shelf. There it was! Tuvalu! I hopped towards the book and opened up like a five-year-old on Christmas. I popped that book off that shelf and started reading.

"Two minutes left!" a guard shouted.

I flipped to the table of contents. In the very back, there was a one page summary of the history of Tuvalu. I ripped out the page later, crumpled it up, and stuffed that piece of paper in my pocket. Then, once I got back to my cell and started writing this, I unfolded it and I am now going to copy down exactly what the page on the history of Tuvalu says:

"Tuvalu is a modern-day commonwealth country consisting of 124 islands and islets, there are 9 main islands, represented by the 9 stars on the flag. Tuvalu means "8 Standing Together" in Tuvaluan since there were only 8 inhabited islands when it was discovered.

Polynesian migration to Tuvalu began about 3,000 years ago from Samoa. When discovered by the Samoans, it was incorporated into the Tu'i Manu'a Confederacy. Later, after the decline of Tu'i Manu'a in the 11th century, Tongans put Tuvalu into their sphere of influence. Four times in the 15th and 16th century, the Tu'i Tonga Empire invaded Tuvalu, two times in Niutao. Then, in the 17th century, Gilbertese warriors from Kiribati invaded two times and failed.

The first European contact with Tuvalu was by Álvaro de Mendaña de Neira in 1568 in a Spanish expedition. Álvaro de Mendaña de Neira passed by the southernmost Tuvaluan island in 1595. In 1764, John Byron charted the islands as the Lagoon Islands. In 1819, British explorers passed by Tuvalu. European whalers started whaling in Tuvalu in 1821.

Christianity was introduced in 1861 by a Christian Deacon from the Cook Islands. Trading in Tuvalu began in Funafuti in the 1850s.

In 1876, Germany and Britain decided to split up the western and central Pacific into spheres of influence. In 1877, the governor of Fiji was given the sphere of influence that included Tuvalu and Kiribati. Starting in 1892, Tuvalu was a British protectorate. In 1916, the administration of the Gilbert and Ellice Islands was established. The United States landed in Tuvalu in 1942 Ellice to prepare for an oncoming invasion from nearby Japanese-owned Kiribati. Many airfields and air bases were built. Many important battles in the War happened in Kiribati, with the American troops coming from Tuvalu. By 1945, the Pacific War had ended and all troops had been deployed elsewhere, one of the leftover military bases was developed into the Funafuti International Airport, which is currently the only airport in Tuvalu.

After the separation of the Administration of the Gilbert and Ellice Islands, Britain gradually transitioned Tuvalu and Kiribati into self-governance. Tuvalu officially gained independence in 1978."

That was a very interesting segment! But, it was super old. The last event in the summary was in 1978! That was one-hundred-fourteen years ago! I could bet you a million dollars that things have changed in the very, very, very long period of one-hundred-fourteen years!

"Let's go! Time's up!" the same guard from before shouted.

It had been another hour of just sitting in my cell, reading. I had been reading the same Tuvalu book I had found when I went to the library. Throughout the book, it mentioned the same exact thing as the summary did, but in a long, expanded, and very over exaggerated way.

Ali walked into the cell, "Whatcha reading?"

"A book about Tuvalu," I responded.

"Ain't that the beer and spirits bar in Rochester?"

"What? How do you know about a restaurant in Rochester?"

"In the library, there was a mystery murder book set in Rochester, NY. It was pretty good. It was obvious who did it though."

"Tuvalu, pronounced *ToohVallOooh*, is a country in the South Pacific."

"And why in the good name of the former sultan of the Neo-Ottoman Empire are you looking at a book about a random country smack-dab in the middle of the insignificant continent of Oceania?"

I looked up at him, "I am trying to find somewhere in the world that is a safehaven. Somewhere where I can go and not abide by the dumb rules of the stupid society in the rest of the world so I can escape."

"That definitely makes sense," Ali rolled his eyes into the very back of his head. "How are you even going to be able to afford plane tickets there? Or do you plan to swim all the way to Tooraloo?"

"I plan to find the money somewhere," I said, hoping not to blow my cover, "somewhere."

"Mmmmmh-kaay," Ali said as he chomped on a cookie snack tube.

"Where did you get that?"

"Turns out I had it in my pocket when I came in this literal prison; it's now kind of crumbly."

"That sounds like you."

"Whatcha reading?" Yuce asked as she entered the cell.

"A book about Tuvalu."

"Tooraloo? That Irish lullaby?"

"*ToohVallOoooh*. A country in Oceania."

"And why in the world are you reading a book about Oceania?"

"Because she wants to escape," Ali chimed in.

"How are you going to pay for a plane ticket? Or are you going to swim all the way to Tooraloo?"

"I'll find the money."

"Where?"

"She's said she'll find it," Ali chimed in again.

We sat in that cell in awkward silence for what seemed like hours. In reality, it was ten minutes. Throughout that time, I continued to read my book about Tuvalu. I didn't learn anything I hadn't learned from the summary. I hoped to find a much newer book about Tuvalu the next time I visited the library. That is if there even was one.

I abruptly set down my book in the middle of a page about World War Two, "What's the plan for escaping this place? Considering that our previous plan was foiled."

"I mean, I do not really want to escape anymore. They have a strenuous amount of effort, especially for Greeks, and I think that it isn't so bad anymore. Plus, I need to serve time in prison to learn from my many major and illegal mistakes. It's just an ethical conundrum I'd rather not entangle myself into," Ali stated, as he crossed his arms and looked down at me.

"I agree. Attempted Assault is a serious crime. In other countries, I would've been given much longer jail time. I should be thankful that I only have so much time in prison. Also, prison HAS improved. With the new standards and regulations, I think I might actually end up becoming an overall good and ethical person from my prison experience," Yuce said in agreement.

"Well, I still have the gun."

"And we both know you still have the gun. Maybe the guard will know soon."

Chapter Seven

I have saved up nine-hundred-forty-two dollars over the past three weeks, including the last weekend I wrote about. Before I started saving up, I spent all my money on things I didn't need. I could've had a significant amount more. Oh well. Today is Saturday and I have arrived at the store. The wind was not as bad this week, especially not today. Instead of the wind howling and the streets bustling, I was greeted this Saturday morning by the sounds of empty streets and stagnant wind. That was when I realized something was up.

As you might know and should probably know, Minnesota has a very large Hmong population, especially the wondrous capital city of St. Paul. Since St. Paul was literally a hop and a skip away from Minneapolis no matter where you are in the city, the Hmong population has spread. Yesterday at night, hundreds of Hmong refugees from Thailand were killed on the Vietnamese-Lao border. Although the Taiwanese Dynasty controls the entire area known as Asia, it was a bit weird to see mention of a Vietnamese government. It is basically another Vietnam War. The US has backed capitalist independence forces that just happen to be in the south, and the Taiwanese Dynasty are backing Communist forces that just happen to be in the north. No matter what, you are no longer allowed in Vietnam unless you are a soldier. There was an influx of Hmong refugees since some more Thai camps had been broken out of by Hmong peoples who were trapped there for decades.

How do you know this, you might ask? Well, I met a very nice Hmong person on my walk to Minneapolis. He was walking toward his home. I asked him why no one was out, and he told me why. Then, he promptly ran away, so that was a wonderful start to the morning.

He had a very interesting accent. Accents have become much evolved; unlike languages, many new accents have come about. There are so many that no one can keep track. He had a very heavy Hmong accent. I happened to have a Hmong accent, but a very light one. He realized that and commented. The rest of my family has a very German accent and a very heavy one at that; it is just another thing that sets me apart from the rest of my family.

I am at the store now. I am one hour into my shift. Not a single customer came during the one hour long time period. It had been pretty boring throughout the entire time. I hoped someone would come so that I could make some money!

It has been another hour. I was one-third done with my shift. Still, no one has come. I wondered if the store was closed. Maybe because of the weird Hmong thing? I couldn't believe that a store would close for some dumb Hmong politics. I needed to make enough money to get out of this place! If no one came here today, I would lose up to fifty-five dollars!

My manager walked into the store. He almost never came here. The last time I saw my manager was when I was hired. He was a five-foot-nine midget with white hair that was legitimately crispy since he used so much hairspray. Of course, he bought the hairspray from the store. He had a small goatee that had enough food crumbs inside of it to make a nice snack. He wore "Trotsky" glasses on the edge of his nose. His age shows in the excess of his wrinkles. He was eighty-five and counting; it was a miracle that he is still alive. Below his oddly long neck, there was a skinny build with lanky arms and long fingers and stubby feet. He wore a neon blue vest over a green fuzzy shirt. His sleeves were rolled up, and his neon colors complemented his dark brown pants. His odd and drawn out look matched the general vibe of the generic Mystery Machine looking convenience store. In some ways, he reminded me of my father. My father would commonly wear "Trotsky" glasses, which he only actually used to read. My mother hated them

Walking into any store, all eyes were locked on him. However, I was the only one there, yet my eyes were still drawn to him. His hair wisped away against the mild wind, strands falling out one by one. He strode himself towards the counter at the end of the store.

"How're sales?" He casually asked as he chewed on a snack tube; the tube's crunchiness was as crunchy as his hair.

81

"Depressing," I said in the most respectful way I could.

Despite the wind being very mild today, it seems like it howled in the silence between responses, "Interesting. My granddaughter's entire family brought themselves over here and, according to their accounts, they spent eighty-four dollars or so? What about that sale?"

His look said everything, voices whispered to me through the wind, telling me not to lie, "Well, that was a great sale; besides that, only two or so more people came before them."

The pause was only nine seconds, but felt like an hour or two as he munched on his tube, "Where are the clothes again?"

I pointed down an aisle, knowing that at least I didn't lie to him about that, "Down there, sir."

He took another bite and stared at me, "Thanks." He started down the aisle, looking around at the products.

That interaction was horrid; nothing I said really made sense. To add to that, my manager was quite creepy. He was dressed like he was the neon convenience store itself.

The manager had left. He had bought a nice neon orange t-shirt for twenty dollars. No other customers have come since then. I am still immeasurably perturbed by my interaction.

My manager has never told me his name. He is a very odd person overall if I haven't already mentioned that twenty-four and a half times. He paid in Angolan Kwanza. What? That country wasn't even allowed out of the country while it was in use. How could he have gotten his hands on it without committing a federal crime? Who just decides to six-thousand-two-hundred and one Angolan Kwanzas and pay their store with them. When I asked him why he was paying with money he knew for a fact that we did not accept in our stores in the state of Minnesota, he responded by saying that I should consider it as a tip and take it for myself.

I guess it was better than stealing it. Oh well, I'll still have to find the ATM in the city center. Maybe that will be my adventure for the day, going to the ATM after my shift is over. I'm almost certainly sure that no one else will come today; everyone is inside because of the Hmong politics.

Three and a half hours into my shift. No sign of anyone coming soon; no one has come so far. I have set up a game with the trash can and some balls. I have a sack of balls and I am trying to shoot all of them into the trash can. I have a spinning chair, so each time I make it, I move back one foot. I am very bad at this game, but I continued to play, for the ball made a very satisfactory sound when I succeeded in throwing the ball inside of the trash can.

ZZZZH! The ball flew from my hand and into the air.

FWOOMP! The ball landed in the trash bag. Success.

CLANK! The ball hit the bottom of the trash can and rolled around.

Four and a half hours in. No one has come. No one will come. My opinion has not changed. My score for the game is three-hundred-fifty-eight of four-hundred and one. I am not doing so well.

ZZZZH!

FWOOMP!

CLANK!

Five and a half hours in. Not much to say. You can probably already tell what happened. I'm doing a bit better. Five-hundred-ninety-nine out of six-hundred and twenty-two

ZZZZH!

FWOOMP!

CLANK!

My shift has ended. Seven-hundred-twelve out of seven-hundred-ninety-nine. I put on my jacket, grabbed the Angolan Kwanzas, and headed out the door, but not before making one more shot.

ZZZZH!
FWOOMP!
CLANK!

I locked the shop behind me. That was a very boring day, it was also a day where I made a mere twenty dollars. The brisk wind and the freezing cold hit me like a hammer against a nail. Minnesota weather; that's just what you have to expect in this messed-up state.

I put up my hood and braced myself for the snow. It was a blizzard. I crunched my boots through the snow. The graceful, yet annoying, crunch of the snow beneath my feet reminded me of the disturbing, and rather irksome, crunch of my manager's alleged "hair."

The wind howled at me fiercely, like it was mad at me. Snow blew in my face. Snow blew everywhere. Snow was everywhere. It had been a while of walking in the right direction, so I looked to my left. There it was! The ATM glowed and shined with its neon lights, and with its radiating heat and warmth, and with its glowing hope that it gave me that I was in the right place.

85

The low hum of the lights drew me in, as I fought against the natural direction of the wind. It headed west, while I yearned to head east. Perhaps my wondrously extravagant lust to head eastward was too much for the blizzard to handle, for it gave in to my pressure.

I walked up to the machine, out of breath from battling the blizzard. I took a nice moment to breathe. I looked up, and the ATM was luckily still there. I readied my other hand in my pocket, the pocket with the money. I clicked the large button that said "START" in all capitals and in three languages. It said the word in German, Hmong, and English. Maybe now was a good time to test my skills at English; I had been practicing pretty diligently and consistently.

My frostbitten hand pressed the START button that was in English. It started talking to me.

Convert, Withdraw, or Deposit?

"Convert."

What currency would you like to receive?

"USD."

You will receive Australian Dollars, is that correct?

"No."

The machine stuttered, *what currency would you like to receive?*

"UNITED STATES DOLLARS," I said very loudly and clearly.

You will receive United States Dollars, is that correct?

"Yes."

Please insert the money you would like to exchange.

I struggled to insert the money, it had become crinkled and dusty while it spent time in my coat pocket.

Please insert the money you would like to exchange.
Please insert the money you would like to exchange.
Please insert the money you would like to exchange.
Please insert the money you would like to exchange.
Please insert the money you would like to exchange.
Please insert the money you would like to exchange.
Please insert the money you would like to exchange.
Please insert the money you would like to exchange.
Please insert the money you would li-

I finally shoved that excessive amount of money into that stupid machine.

Processing.

That freaking machine took its freaking time processing my money as I tapped my foot impatiently.

The currency you have inserted in Angolan Kwanzas, correct?

"Correct."

It buffered, *Thank you for choosing the Bank Of Minneapolis.*

It spat out my money disgracefully. It was exactly twenty dollars. At least it got that detail right. I shoved the money into my coat pocket. On the way back to my house, I had to fight the strong winds that the blizzard had brought. I was late by a significant amount, as the blizzard delayed my speed. Oh well, at least I was still even able to get home that day.

Chapter Eight

How could my prison friends have turned on me? They'd agreed to make a plan with me, and they abandoned me when it failed. I was the one who had the idea and I was the one who was going to carry it out. They turned their backs on me, and nobody would trust someone who just got accused of having a gun, and not one guard heard me tell them what really happened.

Solitary has been wonderful if that was your next question. I wonder if solitary has changed that much since it was first used in prison. All there was was a toilet. It doubled as a chair, or at least that's what the guard said. The toilet was in the center of the depressing room, surrounded by three walls and one constantly guarded prison door to my left.

Could you guess who the guard was? Shegan. The guard was Shegan of all people. So, I couldn't talk to the guard without it being insanely awkward for me and him. That means that it was hours on end, every hour of the days, doing nothing in the middle of the room. I have made many games to play with objects left in my pockets or on the floor.

I was still allowed to keep my three coins. My weird Tuvaluan coin, my Neo-Soviet coin, and my Bermudan coin. I have been playing with the three coins. I flicked one coin through another two coins, and then from another angle. It's similar to how people played games in the 2010s.

I've been flipping the red Neo-Soviet coin I found many, many times. As I am writing this, I am continuing to flip the coin, so I am recording my progress only so far. I have landed tails two-hundred-forty-two times, and one-hundred-thirty-three times. I have landed tails over sixty-four percent of the time. I was beginning to suspect that the coin was weighted on the tails side. The tails side had more colors. The heads side had words etched into it, but the tails side has a Communist insignia of a yellow color which added to the tail side's weight. I've also been flipping the triangular Bermudan coin many times. I flipped it four-hundred times. Heads have been landed on two-hundred and twelve times, while tails have been landed on one-hundred-eighty-eight times. Once I am done flipping the Neo-Soviet coin, I will start flipping the Tuvaluan coin. I suspect that it will be almost equal on both sides, head, and tails.

I am very bored. Very very bored.

"May I have a book?"

"What?" Shegan responded.

"A book for entertainment."

"It's solitary."

"And so?"

"You're not supposed to be entertained."

"Why not?"

"It's solitary confinement."

"You know me. Please be nice."

"Nepotism."

"I just need something to do."

"I do not think you get solitary confinement."

"You know me. I am Gennadiya. I like history and just wanted to study."

"Study what?"

"Language."

"Which language are you studying?"

"Ich studiere Deutsch."

"What?"

"I am studying German."

"Sto studiando Italiano."

"What?"

"I am studying Italian."

"Planning to go there?"

"Paid vacation leave."

"So you understand that it is necessary to study every day?"

"I get it."

"So?"

"I just can not leave the cell."

"Why not?"

"I would lose my job."

"Why?"

"Because according to the official file that is made for you, you are a potential threat to yourself and others. That's why you're in solitary confinement."

"It was Yuce's gun."

"Yeah right."

"I'm not lying."

"Someone in solitary confinement cannot be trusted."

"I'm not lying."

"But you could be, and that is all the prison system cares about."

"Anyone could be lying at any time."

"You know what I meant. Someone with a particularly spotty record cannot be trusted."

"I would just like a dictionary."

Shegan rolled his eyes and then looked back up at me, "Next time I have to go to the library."

"Thank you!"

"Do not mention it."

"Ok," I laughed.

Shegan stared at me with a stern expression, "Do not. It could get me fired. I'm just trying to be nice to you, I get how it feels."

"What do you mean?"

"In 2057, I was arrested in Greece."

"For what?"

"Killing an Albanian representative."

"What?"

"I was born and raised in Albania, and I lived there at that time. I strongly disagreed with Velsa Ismaili."

"Who?"

"I thought you knew your history."

"She was an Albanian liberal who became president in 2046. She was killed by one of her own bodyguards in 2047. She was at a congress meeting discussing Albanian rights under the new Neo-Ottoman rule."

"Do you know what she wanted to do?"

"She wanted to cede all the territory, the population, and the legal rights of Albania to the Neo-Ottoman Empire."

"Did she?"

"She was killed by one of her bodyguards, so no."

"I killed her."

"You were a bodyguard?"

"In my past."

"What made you want to be a prison guard if you already had such a bad experience with prison?"

"I didn't want to be a prison guard."

"Then why are you here? How are you here?"

"Not by choice."

"What do you mean *not by choice*?"

"Most people who go through the Neo-Ottoman or New Greek Empire's prison system end up as guards."

"And the others?"

"They're killed because of the severity of their crime. It's a very few amount of people."

"Why weren't you?"

"I wasn't Velsa's bodyguard. I was her son."

"Why would you kill your own mother?"

"Stepmother."

"Doesn't change anything."

"She was going to make a decision that would kill us all."

"That decision kept the country alive."

"It didn't."

"Why did they consider you a bodyguard?"

"The press liked it better."

"The press liked a bodyguard killing a politician better than her own son killing her?"

"I didn't know that I was her son."

"That makes the story better!"

"The press wanted her death to be remembered insignificantly."

"Why?"

"Everyone just hated her and her politics."

"That doesn't explain-"

"They wanted her to not be remembered."

"Okay, but why did you kill her?"

"You already asked that question."

"And you didn't give me the right answer."

"I was hired."

"By whom?"

"The Albanian government itself."

"The Albanian government hired someone to kill their president?"

"They hired the right person."

"Nobody would expect Velsa's son to kill his mother."

"Stepmother."

"Doesn't matter."

"Also, I was always with her."

"Makes sense."

"Why weren't you killed?"

"My crime was too serious. They wanted to punish me by constantly making me be with people so insane that they needed solitary confinement. I have to constantly be by random people who were so awfully horrid that they ended up in the New Greek prison."

"Working in prison as a guard is worse than being killed?"

"According to the Neo-Ottoman government. And according to the New Greek government."

"Do you agree with that?"

"Yes."

"So, I'm that horrible to be with?"

"Indeed. I'll remember to get you the book, OK. Just stop asking questions about my past?"

"Thank you again for the book. I'll stop asking questions about your past, OK? I'll stop."

"What are you writing?"

"I'm writing down the entirety of this conversation."

"Why?"

"School project."

"And you're continuing it in prison?"

"Yep."

"Impressive."

I have been studying German for hours. I feel like I know every word there is to know. I am tired of German. I am excited about the next language. I speak six languages: Turkish, Greek, English, Hindi Turkish, Bosnian, and now German. I have become fluent in German after reading the dictionary so much. What should my next language be? Italian, maybe? Albanian? So I could speak to Shegan more? Serbian? So I could escape to Serbia?

That brings up a good question. Where would I go once I have escaped from this stupid prison? Istanbul? No, I would be caught by Greek police or armies and killed. That's also why I can not reveal myself as the heir to the throne of the entire New Greek Empire. Any city in Turkey is off of the list. Any city in all of the New Greek Empire is off of the list of places to go. I would get caught by Greek police or armies. That puts most of the cities near me off the list. I would have to go somewhere where there was a major airport. Besides Istanbul! Besides Damascus! Besides Tashkent (if it is still owned by the New Greek Empire when I get there)! And besides New Delhi! I need to go somewhere the New Greek Empire isn't! The New Greek Empire would kill me! What about a place NEAR the New Greek Empire? Bosnia? Bosnian Herzegovina? The SRPSKA Free State? The last one is a no, for it is a part of the Neo-French Empire. I do not speak French. Bosnian Herzegovina is still a somewhat violent area. Bosnia is a very intriguing destination, it seems to make sense.

Bosnia has a major city. It is a tier two city, otherwise known as a population center. It has a population of eight-hundred-fifty-three-thousand and eight-hundred-eighty-two. That city is Sarajevo. I have been there, and it is quite the fun and interesting city. Plus, I speak Bosnian. And, in due time, I might speak Serbian as well. Sarajevo has a major airport. All major cities have airports in Europe and South America (only because there are only two major cities in South America), but Asia and North America do not go by that rule.

I have written down a conversation down in this entry, for I want to remember this for a long time. Shegan lied. The two people involved in this conversation thought that I was asleep.

"Is she sleeping?" A guard taking over the shift for Shegan asked.

"Yeah," Shegan responded.

"How was your first shift?"

"Hilarious!"

"What did you do this time?"

"Gennadiya thought that I was put in prison for killing Velsa Ismaili and became a guard because my crime was too severe."

"What?" He chuckled.

"She believed it."

"Yeah right."

"I was her son and killed her because I was hired by the Albanian government."

"That sounds crazy enough to be true in this modern-day world."

"She's crazy enough to believe it."

"Why would you get hired by the prison if you were previously convicted?"

"It makes absolutely NO sense."

"She has amnesia or something?"

"She thinks she is Gennadiya, a refugee from Georgia."

"I kind of feel bad."

"You know who she really is though?"

"Yeah. It's crazy that she would shoot a major Greek politician."

"How was that helping her to stay on the low? I mean, you wouldn't want to get caught. But, she still committed a major crime right after she knew that she was going to get killed."

"Just wait two weeks."

"Two weeks?"

"Yup. And then the New Greek Empire will finally have control."

"We should at least be nice to her while she is even alive."

"Sure." The other guard took the place and started his shift.

As I said, I was not actually asleep while all of that unfolded before me. Shegan had lied. I had lied. They knew I had lied. Had Ali or Yuce known I had lied? How had they known I had lied? Maybe a DNA test? Maybe because I have a few portraits and photographs in the media?

Well, they knew who I was, and I can not change that now. All I can do is think of a way to escape. I do not have my gun anymore, it was taken by authorities. I couldn't risk taking on someone with a gun if I didn't have one, they would absolutely kill me, and it would be no competition. While I was contemplating my life and how I'd get out of here, someone dropped a pineapple by my cell door.

I guess it was about dinnertime. I, of course, after so long being secluded from society, have no sense of time whatsoever. It could be morning, and that pineapple could be breakfast. A knife plopped down next to the pineapple.

"Cut the pineapple," Shegan looked down at me, "That's your breakfast."

So it was breakfast. Interesting. But, how does one go about slicing a pineapple? I remember my father teaching me at a young age when we had nothing else we could possibly have for breakfast. First I cut the stem off. The pineapple was very hard, almost as if it wasn't ripe. Then, I cut the crown off as well. I screwed up the first time and the crown was still mostly on. I repositioned my knife and tried again. I almost cut myself. Success.

Next came the even harder part. I turned the remaining pineapple onto its side. I shaved off the outer edges with the edge of my knife. I was quite bad at this, and cut in far too deep every single time. After that tediously repetitive step, I had to remove the eyespots. There were many. I positioned my knife to cut diagonally in, and the repositioned it to cut diagonally out, creating a V shape that would get rid of eyespots more efficiently.

I turned the pineapple onto its left side, the side it was on when I first cut it. I sliced the wheel into disks. Pineapple disks. Fun breakfast, but I got it because they most likely did not have anything else. I had cut them far too deep, but there was still enough.

However, this monotonous and slightly dangerous task was too much work for a simple breakfast.

But, there was a substantial benefit. I now am in the possession of a weapon I could use many ways to get out of here, otherwise known as a knife. At the night shift, when the guard usually falls asleep, I could cut the bars and make a run for it. The bars on the cell were not very sturdy at all, they could be easily broken like a small twig using a knife.

Yet, like before, I was incredibly nervous. But why was I so nervous if the plan was so simple and foolproof?

I woke up with a craving for cheesecake. Sweet, sweet cheesecake. It was quite off, but I believe I was dreaming of a memory in which I headed to an actual cheesecake factory with my father on my birthday. It's quite yummy.

Also, I woke up with doubts about my mission. Were the bars really thin or fragile that I could simply cut through them? If so, was the knife really strong enough to cut them? If they were not fragile enough, then the knife would definitely not be strong enough.

Why was I even breaking out? I committed a very serious crime, and now, I have to pay. Even if that means me dying. It's just the right thing to do. I am a very ethical person, or was I? If I was ethical, why had I shot someone just because I did not agree with them on politics?

Where would I go if I broke out? Well, first, out of the prison. Then, to a bank. After that, to a cab. Through the cab, to Sarajevo, and then to their airport. Then, I would buy tickets to Tuvalu. If not Tuvalu, the Taiwanese Dynasty, for they would protect me as a hostage as bait against the New Greek Empire. That would be an okay idea. But, I would still be forced back into the same dumb society. Well, I will see where I end up going once I ask for tickets. Finally, through the airplane, I will arrive in Tuvalu, and I will have found a safehaven.

That is if I could get past Shegan at night.

Chapter Nine

It is a rainy day. Not literally, but figuratively. It is a snowy day. Still the same results though. On a snowy day, everyone has to stay in and do nothing. All of the convenience stores are closed. It is a very boring concept. Fun fact: In Minnesota, there has not been an official rainy day for five decades, instead there have been snowy days. It's not as fun. Rather than there being puddles to splash in the next day, the snow is built up against the very walls and doors of your house for three weeks on end, leaving you to wonder when it will end.

School is closed as well. The museum is closed too. Everything is closed. So, I decided to make a To-Do List regarding my mission of escaping my society and finding a safehaven. Here it is:

1. Save up the proper amount of money, currently one-thousand-two-hundred and eight dollars out of thirty-two-hundred dollars
2. Escape house - can be done after museum job, after convenience store job, or after school. Ideally after convenience store job on weekends.
3. Get to the airport, will probably take a while, and should probably remember to bring snack tubes and/or meal tubes. However, food might be provided on the plane or at the airport.
4. Get tickets, remember to use lower voice.

5. Backup, if Tuvalu isn't able to be flown to, then I will go to Nauru, even though it is uninhabited.
6. Fly to Tuvalu! This step is self-explanatory.
7. Paradise!

The money might be a problem. I still have one-thousand-nine-hundred-ninety-two dollars left if the price even costs that much. I should totally go to the airport and check the price so that I know how much I ACTUALLY need to save up. The snow will go away soon enough. Also, now or next time when I go to the airport, I might even meet someone who is also going to Tuvalu. It is a very unlikely event; there is almost no chance of it happening. But, I can hope.

It has been one week. I have made no money in one whole week, and now, I am going to the airport. My day at the convenience store was fun and successful. Sixty-nine dollars have been inserted into my bank account. One-thousand-two-hundred-seventy-seven out of thirty-two hundred. Getting slowly closer. Many customers came just to have human interaction after a week of spending all of their time inside. They left large tips. I took only seventy-seven percent of the money that the convenience store got today.

I trudged through the treacherous snow, going to the ATM. It was very tedious, and the snow was worse than the last time I went to the ATM. The snow went up higher, the snow was thicker, and the wind blew harder westwards than I could have ever imagined.

I got to the ATM. I chose English again. I have become pretty good at speaking English, despite all of the dumb and hard-to-follow rules. It seems as though every other word in the entire English language breaks a rule of the English language that was earlier established.

Convert, Withdraw, or Deposit?

"Deposit."

What currency shall you be depositing in?

I had gotten two currencies today. CAD and USD, "USD."

You will deposit in USD, correct?

It actually got it right, "Correct."

How much are you depositing?

"Forty-six dollars."

Not a valid number. How much are you depositing?

Of course, I ran into a problem, "FORTY-SIX DOLLARS."

Forty-six dollars, is that right?

The machine sounded very appalled, which took me for a surprise, "Yes."

Please insert the money you would like to deposit.

I struggled to take the money out of my pocket, once again. I fished around in my left pocket. Before, I had sorted them into USD and CAD. The CAD in the right pocket, and USD in the left pocket.

Please insert the money you would like to deposit.
Please insert the money you would like to deposit.
Please insert the money you would like to deposit.
Please insert the money you would like to deposit.
Please insert the money you would like to deposit.
Please insert the money you would like to deposit.
Please insert the money you would like to deposit.
Please insert the money you would like to deposit.
Please insert the money you w-

I finally shut that dumb machine up and inserted the money.

Processing.
Then, after a good minute, *please enter the password.*

I entered my password into the tricky machine.

Processing.
Deposited.
Would you like to make another deposit?

"Yes."

What currency shall you be depositing in?

"CAD."

You will deposit in CAD, right?

"Correct."

How much are you depositing?

"Twenty-three dollars."

Twenty-three dollars, is that right?

"Yes."

Please insert the money you would like to deposit

Please insert the money you would like to deposit.

Please insert the money you would like to deposit.

Please insert the money you would like to deposit.

Please in-

I finally shut that up.

Processing.

Please enter the password.

I entered the password yet again.

Processing.

Deposited.

Would you like to make another deposit?

"No."

Thank you for using The Bank Of Minneapolis.

Goodness gracious, that machine was unbelievably annoying. Who had invented these??

I trudged through the snow yet again. I was going to the airport. I was going to the airport to check prices on a flight to somewhere where I do not even know if it exists anymore.

I arrived at the airport. It had been a very long walk. I have used up all of my snack tubes. I'll have to buy more tomorrow at the convenience store before school or after the museum job. The airport was the biggest building I had ever seen. Airports are huge! Planes flying in and out! It's insane! It was also quite overwhelming; it took me a second before I could head in.

I headed in through the side entrance and looked around. To my left, there was a sign that said Customer Service. To my front, there was a sign that said Boarding Flights.

To my right, there was a sign that said Connecting Flights. I headed on over to customer service. It was quite a busy airport, everyone was bustling about and I could barely see over the crowd.

I finally arrived at customer service. No one was in line. Which made sense, considering the fact that no one was at the desk. Although, there was a pile of maps that seemed to be of the airport itself. I picked one up. It was poorly drawn. I compared that map to my surroundings. Nope, of course, it wasn't accurate. It said that I was in the landing lot. Wow! This airport must have been renovated a lot! I was absolutely and horribly lost.

I walked over past the hall between connecting flights and boarding flights. Then, there were landing flights right in front of me. To my left, a hall, to my right, a security station. I went down the hallway. It was shops galore. Convenience stores, medicinal pharmacies, and stores selling things tourists would want! A passport store! A bank! A coat store! A hat store! A ticket-pricing station!

The ticket-pricing station. I ran over there. I was out of breath by the time I got there. I caught my breath and opened the heavy metal door. It creaked open as I was met with a silent room with two computer stations. The quietness of the room I had entered was in stark contrast to the business of the airport.

I went over to the computer closest to me, the one on the left. There was a START button in green with ten different languages: English, German, Hmong, Spanish, French, Turkish, Taiwanese Mandarin, Portuguese, Vietnamese, and Russian. I chose English, yet again.

You have chosen English. You are in Minneapolis in the
Minneapolis- St. Paul Airport. Welcome. Start by saying your destination
First, say the country.

"TooVallOooh," I enunciated.

Did you say Tuvalu?

"Yes."

Now, what city in that country would you like to go to?

"Asau," I said, only because it sounded the most interesting in the
book.

I am sorry, we do not provide flights to Asau. In the country of
Tuvalu, we provide flights only to the city of Funafuti. My apologies for the
inconvenience. Would you like pricing on flights to Funafuti, Tuvalu?

I was not disappointed, "Yes, please."

Do you have a date in mind for the departure?

"No."

Okay. I will calculate the average. While you are waiting, here is a
factoid about Tuvalu. Did you know that Tuvalu's name means eight
standing together in the local tongue of Tuvaluan?

The average price for a flight from Minneapolis, Minnesota, in the
continent of North America to Funafuti, Tuvalu, in Oceania is twenty-eight-
hundred-thirty-six United States Dollars and fifty-three cents. Would you
like the price converted to another currency?

"No."

Okay. Would you like to know useful information such as the languages and currency?

Woah! This machine was super useful, but time-consuming, "Yes."

The official languages of the country of Tuvalu, as of January 2092, are Tuvaluan and English. The currencies of the country of Tuvalu are the Tuvaluan Dollar and the Australian Dollar. Tālofa is how you say hello. Have a good day and we hope your trip goes well!

I left the room, flabbergasted at how much information I had gotten out of one visit to this machine. I think that Operation Tuvalu will succeed.

The walk home was very difficult. The snow's crunches became deafening after a certain amount of time. The wind has calmed down after hours of it riling up. After an exhaustingly long and tedious walk, I ended up at one of the last places I wanted to be, home.

I walked into the house and was met with a sign that read: HAPPY BIRTHDAY! It surely wasn't my birthday. We have already established this. I looked down on the ground, and there was a Mexican Peso. Cool! It was from 2017, so it was quite old. It looked like a Euro. On what I think to be the front, there was gold, with two dollars etched into it surrounded by a silver edge that had Mayan symbols, which made the whole coin look just like a Mayan calendar.

Suddenly, someone yelled my name.

"Austin! Where are you! We have been waiting for you! It's Sydney's birthday today! You were late!" An unknown voice shouted from the living room.

"Sorry," I shouted back as I took off my winter coat and shoes.

I walked into the room and looked around, "We were just doing presents, we just finished Robert's gift to Sydney. It was a very fancy pen for calligraphy and/or cartography. Where is your gift?"

What? It was someone's birthday? Nobody told me until now! I pulled out my Mexican Peso from out behind my back, "Here it is. It's a really rare Mexican Peso from all the way back in 2017."

I awaited their response, they would either call me lazy and hate it, or maybe, possibly, in an unlikely scenario, love it. Sydney took the Mexican Peso and inspected it, "Wow! Thanks, Austin. This is pretty cool. The symbols on the outer edges are pretty interesting. Thanks!"

Crisis averted.

Mondays suck. They always have and always will. This is my first time bringing my journal to school. I've stopped by in the bathroom in between classes. I should not be writing in here. I just need a break from all of the stress and all of the dumb and useless facts they try to shove into your head.

Today, in history class, otherwise known as Social Studies, I asked the teacher about Tuvalu. That did not go well. The teacher immediately scoffed after hearing my question and the entire class laughed, thinking I asked if a restaurant in Rochester was a country.

Then, after no one believed me, I asked the teacher for an atlas. It turns out that the school can not afford an atlas. Everyone continued to laugh at my expense; it was humiliating.

As soon as I went out of the bathroom, I was confronted by someone whose name later turned out to be Jack. The interaction went something like this:

"Oy, the bell rang five minutes ago, if I were you, I'd take my bathroom break during lunch."

"Duly noted," I tried to get past him.

"He moved towards me, "Listen, I know that Tuvalu is an actual place."

I stopped in my tracks, "What?"

"Found an old stamp."

"How?"

"I used to work at the post office near the ATM in the city center."

"It's real?"

"As far as I can tell."

"Do you know anything else about it?"

"No, just found a stamp."

"Then why did you come to tell me?"

"Just wanted to make sure you knew that you were right."

"Do you want to escape to Tuvalu?"

He briskly walked away backward from me and then ran off, only after saying "I do not have that much free time. I have to get to class. My name is Jack. Good luck on your adventure; you'll need it."

It's too bad he wouldn't join me. Maybe, just maybe, I'll meet someone at the airport. I just want someone to join me on this quest, just so I am not entirely alone in Tuvalu.

Chapter Ten

I am in Sarajevo as I am writing this. I made it! It was quite the adventure.

First, I had to break out of the cell. I had the pineapple knife from before, and it was strong enough to break down the cell bars. The trick was to start in the afternoon. I slowly sawed at each cell bar any chance I could grab when the guard wasn't looking. It took a while, but it was worth it. Every single cell bar was halfway sawed-through by night, and the guards couldn't see, because I sawed parts off on my side. From the front, the cell bars looked normal. But from the back, you could see that a major dent had been made in them, and that one more hack at it using the knife would make them come toppling down.

Then came the nighttime. Shegan was guarding, as I had expected. I woke up after a couple hours of fake sleeping to convince the guards I was asleep, and went to work. I sawed the bars that were furthest away from where Shegan was. I hacked at the cell bars quietly, and it took a decent amount of time before I could pry the bars from their glue that was holding them on. This cell was built very cheaply. The sharp bars made a very loud noise as they fell to the floor, but that never happened, because, despite the cell bars' weight, I was able to catch them. I slipped through the bars by holding in my stomach.

I made sure not to forget my journal. I hopped by all of the guards who were sleeping and out of the door. I quietly tiptoed down the stairs, and headed for the exit. It was locked. All of this for nothing? No. I retraced my steps back to Shegan. I knew he had a key. Idiot! He had held his key in his hands, as if he was about to use them. I slid the key ring out of his hands and then quietly, yet quickly went back through the doors and down the stairs until I got to the exit. I used the process of elimination to test which key would finally end up unlocking the door. The process of elimination tested my limited patience.

Finally, I was free! Right? Wrong! I kept the key ring with all of its useful keys and jogged out towards the gate. The process of elimination tested my patience again, and at that point, the process of elimination had tested my very limited patience two times too many in one day. I hopped over the fence. To anticipate your next question, yes, I did keep the keys. I ran across the city. It was my first time seeing where I was. Those idiots have put me in the Istanbul prison. No wonder it was so luxurious! I ran through the city, looking for a cellar near a pile of wood on a pillar.

I was looking for one of the signal spots. Luckily, the doors were made of wood, so that the flame from the signal would burn down the door or something crazy like that. Before the New Greek Empire took over the Neo-Ottoman Empire's capital of Istanbul, the cellar doors were metallic. Those dumb Greeks. Instead of using a key, I kicked down that door like a common madman.

I knew this cellar. This was the cellar I had left my peasant clothes in. Wait, I hear you ask, didn't you already use your peasant clothes before? A proper girl can never have enough backups. I changed faster than I ever thought I could in my life. I slipped into my so-called costume, and I was looking like a peasant already. I ran out of the cellar immediately.

I ran toward the city center, hoping to get to the Istanbul ATM. I could withdraw a bunch of money, if not all of my money, I would take it out in Bosnian Convertible Marks so I could buy plane tickets once I got to Sarajevo. Of course, I can not go to the Istanbul airport, for I would be spotted and promptly killed. In Sarajevo, nobody would know who I was, as they are too busy fighting a war against Bosnian Herzegovina. I could also just take out a card, but then my name would be displayed on the front of the card for all to see.

I arrived at the Istanbul ATM. I made sure it was on the lowest volume possible, so no one would wake up. Surprisingly, there was a bag next to the ATM. It said that it was for collecting money if someone needed it and that it should be returned. Yeah, I was never returning that.

I clicked the START button. It had ten languages: Turkish, Greek, Turkish Urdu, Hindi Turkish, Serbian, Updated Modern Standard Arabic, Albanian, Russian, English, and Taiwanese Mandarin. I chose Turkish.

Hello. Convert, withdraw, or deposit?

"Withdraw."

You would like to withdraw, correct?

"Correct."

How much would you like to withdraw?

I did a quick conversion, "forty-three-thousand-six-hundred-eighty-four Turkish Liras."

You would like to withdraw Forty-three-thousand-six-hundred-eighty-four Turkish Liras, correct?

"Correct."

What currency would you like to receive?

"Bosnian Convertible Marks."

You would like to receive Bosnian Convertible Marks, correct?

"Correct."

You will receive twelve-thousand-seven-hundred-fifty-three Bosnian Convertible Marks. Please enter your password.

I entered my password of the emergency credit card I had. It had exactly twelve-thousand-seven-hundred-fifty-three Bosnian Marks on it. I was about to withdraw all of my money.

You are aware that you are about to withdraw your entire savings, would you like to cancel?

"No."

Processing.

Thank you for choosing the Istanbul Bank, the official bank of the Neo-Ottoman Empire!

The ATM spat out my money, and I held my bag up to the thing that spewed out my money. I did not have time to check if all of the money was there. I ran off to the airport. I ended up walking, for it would have been quite the long run. I covered my face and went over to the taxi section. I constantly looked away from the security cameras that faced me.

I hailed a taxi and jumped into the first one I saw.

"My name is Raphail, and I am your taxi driver for this trip. Where would you like to go?" the taxi driver asked rather happily.

"Sarajevo," I responded bluntly.

Flabbergasted, the driver responded, "That's one-thousand-one-hundred-sixty-two kilometers! That will cost you a pretty penny!"

I dumped my bag of cash in the driver's seat, "Just go."

The driver stared at the money for a good second, he was seemingly in disbelief, "Okay then, would you like to go the route through Greece or through Serbia? The Greek route is longer."

"The Serbian route."

The man finally started driving. It was a long drive. By long, I mean interminably long. Fourteen hours and seventeen minutes. Good thing I had stolen a couple snack tubes from the guards as well. Also, at the airport, I got some meal tubes. Everything had turned out perfectly. Unless, this taxi driver finds out who I am, which is unlikely taking into account how very naive he is.

119

During the drive, he was not talkative. Except, for one conversation which I was able to write down.

We were ten and a half hours in to the drive by this point, when Raphail turned his head, "I'm sorry, why are you going to Sarajevo through a taxi cab?"

I looked up from my book, "Cheaper than most flights."

Raphail looked confused, but carried on driving. "So, where are you from originally?"

I hadn't had proper human contact in a while, so I decided to engage in a bit of friendly conversation. "Istanbul. Lived there my whole entire life."

Raphail delved into the conversation as well. "Well, I was born in Kavala, in mainland Greece. What takes you to Sarajevo?"

"Family," I lied.

"Cool. Hey, I never got your name. What is it?"

I just realized that in the midst of the conversation, I had revealed where I was actually from, yet I had been acting like Gennadiya Petrov out of habit. I had to come up with a new backstory for a fake person, and quickly, so I thought of a Russian name, as I am now someone who has lived in Istanbul her whole entire life, yet is Russian by descent somehow, "My name is Siyansky Rasim Innokentievich. It is quite the pleasure to meet you Raphail."

"You have a beautiful accent."

"I get it from my father's side, I am Russian by descent, but my family moved here once Russia was taken over. Now I am going to see family in Sarajevo to see if I can stay with them."

"Mmkay."

"You know, Bosnia has a great flag."

"Indeed. It's odd how they kept some of the same symbols after the Neo-Ottoman invasion, and also kept the colors of their old flag."

"I consider myself an honorary vexillologist."

"Me as well."

"What is your favorite flag then?"

"The flag for the French territory of Andorra while it was still colonized."

"I remember that, it has not been so long since they were still a tiny colony. Weren't they the last colony decolonized by the Neo-French Empire?"

"Indubitably. What is your favorite flag?"

"The current flag of the South Brazilian Free State."

"That is indeed quite the nice flag."

"Excited to see your family?"

"What?"

"Are you excited in any way to see your family?"

"Sorry. Did not hear you the first time. The answer is no. They're quite the unpleasant people. But I'll have to be very pleasing so that they offer me a place to stay in Sarajevo."

"Oh."

"How's your family?"

"They are doing okay. We have a reunion later this week. You probably know my family as a matter of fact, my cousin is the one and only Antonis Melis."

I gasped, "Really?"

"Yep."

"Wow! That's impressive."

"Yeah, it's fun being the royal family, we get tons of benefits."

"Then why are you working a job that pays a cent more than minimum wage if you get benefits?"

"Human interaction," he said after a longer than needed pause.

"Interesting."

That is where that very awkward conversation ended. I was in the car with the cousin of my enemy for fourteen hours and seventeen minutes. I could not believe that Raphail the taxi driver was related to Antonis Melis, the ruler of the entirety of the New Greek Empire! On our drive, we stopped two times. We stopped to get a drink and a newspaper the first of the two times.

The drink was fine, it was carbonated water with a mixture of excessive amounts of sugar and food coloring, otherwise known as soda, or pop. The newspaper caught my eye. There, in big letters, on the front page were the auspicious words: *Bosnian Convertible Mark's Value Soars in the Midst of a War! An Economic Miracle for Bosnia and its Economy!*

I read through the article eagerly. I ripped out the page and put it in my journal below:

Bosnian Convertible Mark's Value Soars in the Midst of a War!

An Economic Miracle for Bosnia and its Economy!

Today, the Bosnian population woke up to a treat! The Bosnian Convertible Mark's value skyrocketed over three point two percent! However, not only was this a treat to the economy, but it was also a treat to the war. The Bosnian-Herzegovinian War started in 2052 as a result of the Bosnian Reformation. Since the beginning of this decades-long war, the currencies of both countries have plummeted. After the start of the war, Bosnian Herzegovina opted to make their own currency, known as the Herzegovinian Mark. Currently, the Herzegovinian Mark's value has hit the record lowest it has been at in twenty years! Meanwhile, Bosnia is having fun as its currency's value went to an all-time high.

Analysts have speculated about the cause of this unprecedented change. It may have something to do with the influx of trading with the Kingdom of Bosnia, after they started importing large amounts of weapons and ammunition from the Neo-French Empire. In exchange, they have given many things, yet nothing has improved their economy as much as exporting recycled metal scraps. That's right! After bombs flew over the country all those decades ago, they sat there for a long time. While many have rust, more recent bomb shells are intact. These shells have been used as scrap metal for producing much needed ATM machines in mainland France. After a banking scandal in 2031, all of the ATM's in the country were removed or destroyed. Sixty-two years without a single ATM in the country! The Neo-French Empire has invested an excessive amount of money to get the scrap metal, and they are not looking at stopping.

Also, they have inspired the nearby ruined lands and countries of Scandinavia to start doing the same. Next week, the Bosnian Kingdom will start shipments of scrap metal to twenty-one minor Norwegian kingdoms and confederacies, and three Swedish states, including the infamous authoritarian Swedish state known as Upper Gotland. It is predicted that these investments, if continued properly will raise the Bosnian Convertible Mark's value by three point two percent every week or so. It will be exciting to see if this newfound wealth affects the outcome of battles, and maybe even the Bosnian-Herzegovinian War itself!

Oh, how that news article changed my temperament. I was much happier knowing I would have an excessive amount of excess money. Plus, I would actually have enough money to pay the taxi driver. On our second stop, I got another newspaper. This was a day after the previous newspaper

124

was dated. The headline caught my eye for a very different reason, a very unfortunate reason. I tore the article out and have pasted it in my journal below:

Heir to Throne of the Neo-Ottoman Empire, Suspected Dead, Found in Prison

The heir to the throne of the Neo-Ottoman Empire was "killed" in an attack weeks ago, in late December. Her name was Maurie Osman, the daughter of the former ruler of the Neo-Ottoman Empire, Izzet Osman. Izzet was killed that same day, less than seventeen minutes after Maurie was "killed." At Dimos Vassallos's speech, an unknown bystander shot the Greek politician after he finished his speech. Less than a week ago, a young Georgian refugee by the name of Gennadiya Petrov was admitted into the Istanbul Prison. She was arrested for murder.

Gennadiya Petrov is Maurie Osman. Today, she was put into solitary confinement after it was revealed she had a gun. Gennadiya, or should I say Maurie, claimed the gun was belonging to someone by the name of Yuce Catli. Yuce Catli denied these claims. This means that Maurie Osman shot the former ruler of the New Greek Empire, Dimos Vassallos, and she is still alive.

It is suspected that Maurie Osman shot Dimos Vassallos and, when arrested, claimed she was a Georgian refugee by the name of Gennadiya

Petrov. The DNA tests begged to differ. She is set to be executed in two weeks. The execution would be held by Antonis Melis, and will be open to the public.

If Maurie or Gennadiya escapes solitary confinement, then she will have the right to claim the Neo-Ottoman, or should I say New Greek, throne. However, if she is still within the country and within custody, she will not be able to be a ruler. In the Neo-Ottoman Empire, there was a strict rule that no one who has ever served jail time may sit in the throne. Luckily, this rule has carried over to the New Greek Empire. If she leaves the country, she can no longer be held against for her jail time, and she will be able to rule the New Greek Empire, despite her not being within the country because of a loophole in the New Greek constitution.

During her time in jail, she was in a cell with Yuce Catli and Ali Ertugrul. They knew that Gennadiya was really Maurie Osman. They were promised that they would be set free if they were able to put Gennadiya, or Maurie, into solitary confinement. However, neither of them needed to, as Gennadiya, or Maurie was already armed when she came into the prison. Yuce reported this to an officer, but she will not be set free, for Maurie's confinement is not a result of Yuce's actions.

Maurie is still in solitary confinement at the time of writing this article.

That article was very hard to read. I wonder what newspapers will say when they find out I have escaped. Hopefully, they do not end up finding out any more than that. Enough about the newspapers, because I reached Sarajevo an hour and forty-five minutes after finishing that article. I was dropped off at the Sarajevo airport. The conversation I had with Raphail regarding his pay was quite awkward, and I can unfortunately remember every word of it.

"This is Sarajevo International Airport. Your stop," Raphail stated.

I jumped up and went to the door of the cab, it was locked, "The door is locked, Raphail."

"You didn't pay," Raphail looked down and tapped the steering wheel, "And there is a large bag of money in the front seat. You owe me about three-thousand-one-hundred and twelve dollars for the fare and the initial cost."

"Then take three-thousand-one-hundred and twelve dollars from the sack," I commanded Raphail.

"It just might take me awhile."

"I can wait for a while."

He ended up counting out all of the money he needed, plus an impressively generous tip. He left me at the side entrance of the Sarajevo International Airport. I spoke fluent Bosnian, so it was no trouble speaking to others. The first thing I did was go on a major shopping spree.

127

I needed supplies and necessary items, since I brought none from my wondrously fun time in prison. Also, I had a sack of money, and it was the local currency. Plus, there were stores as far as the eye could see.

I bought a backpack first. Then, I went to the freezer and shoved two shelves worth of meal and snack tubes into my front pocket. I also got a meal juice, as I was pretty hungry. The funny thing is, that part of the shopping spree barely made a dent, as meal and snack tubes are very cheap in bulk. After that, I nabbed some essential supplies, such as a toothbrush, clean clothes, and a comb. Following that, I bought exactly seventeen books. Five dictionaries, and twelve for entertainment. I made sure to get a dictionary in Tuvaluan, which was hard to find. I had to go to nine different stores before I found one.

Finally, I bought a telegram. That was, by far, the most expensive thing I bought, but I knew I needed it. Plus, I still had enough money to buy plane tickets to Tuvalu for two people. Also, the value of Bosnian Convertible Marks skyrocketed, so prices plummeted.

When my shopping spree came to an end, I went up to the tickets desk. Once it became my turn, the worker and I had a very interesting conversation.

"How may I help you today?" the worker asked, as she typed on her computer rapidly.

"I would like tickets to Tuvalu."

"Let me check on that," She turned back to her computer and searched it up.

"Thank you."

"I'm sorry, but, unfortunately, we do not have tickets to Tuvalu until the next one, which is in nine days."

"How many days?"

"Nine." She looked down at me, with her glasses pulled down on her nose, disapprovingly.

"W-"

"Next in line!" she shouted angrily.

Chapter Eleven

One-thousand-five-hundred-twenty-four United States Dollars and forty-seven cents out of twenty-eight-hundred-thirty-six United States Dollars and fifty-three cents. Fifty-three point seven-four-four-one-eight-seven percent! I hope that I get a large influx of cash, because boy do I need it! I am about to head out to the ATM. It is Sunday. This is before my job starts. I'll write again when I have time.

I arrived at the scarring scene unprepared for what I was about to see. Smoke rose from the debris, calling out to all who wanted to see a commotion. A crowd had congregated in front of it, and I pushed through them to see. I was not prepared. After I pushed through the rambunctious crowd, I came face to face with my future that was up in flames.

The ATM was decimated. The debris left over was smoking from the fire. It had been bombed. An act of terrorism. The wall behind it was left with a burning hole to reminisce of what used to be in front of it. The bombshell was lying adjacent to the debris.

Next to the ATM was an officer. A police officer. I hadn't seen one of those since 2081. He was holding back the crowd, explaining what had happened. All I knew is that it was bombed.

"Sir? What happened?" I asked innocently.

"It's a mess. Someone bombed it or somethi'. Act o' terrorism," the Texan sounding police officer responded.

If he could enunciate a single word properly, that would make it easier to actually understand him. "By whom?"

"Hmongs, I bet," he said, halfheartedly paying attention to my questions.

"Is that known for a fact?"

"Listen kid, just get out o' her'. You'll get kille' if ya' stay ou' her' fu' too long," he said, hoping I would leave.

"Are they going to rebuild?"

"Not 'til they fin' ou' who did i'."

"Where's the next nearest one?"

"Prolly' in Toledo."

Toledo. Six-hundred-sixty-nine miles away from Eden Prairie, Minnesota. That's a long way away. Goes through five states on the fastest route. That would be quite a long walk to go to an ATM. That would be quite a lot of effort just to get to an ATM. If I walked there, people would probably be very suspicious. Maybe, if I went on the weekend, I could say I was staying at a friend's house and then hitchhike all the way to the northwestern Ohioan city of Toledo. So, there goes my plan. Without an

ATM, I would not be able to withdraw my money. Without my money, I would never be able to buy a plane ticket to Tuvalu. I would never be able to find a safehaven. I would never be able to escape society.

On the contrary side, or the optimistic side, I just found a bag of money. You read that sentence correctly. I found a giant sack of money. All CAD. Where did I find it? In the secret room. YES, there IS a secret room. I was going to the closet of the convenience store, and I found a secret room. The door to the closet opened to the left, and covered the hidden door. Since people mostly only grabbed stuff off of the shelf, and then closed the door, no one closed the door behind them to find the door hidden just to the left. The room was just large enough that the door on the left could fit. When I went in to the closet, I closed the door behind me, as I needed to look through the stuff in the closet. I turned on the measly light bulb attached to the ceiling by one last wire that was soon to fall off, and I looked to my direct left, and saw the secret door.

Me being the curious jerk I am, I decided to snoop inside the meta closet. Hidden closet IN a closet. Ingenious. I opened the door inward, and walked into the meta closet. Yes, I will continue to call the room behind the door to my direct left in the miniature closet a *meta closet*. It is a perfect name and you can not stop me. You can not stop me whoever is reading this, also why are you reading my journal?

Anyway, I opened the meta closet and came face to face with an empty stone room with a lightbulb in an even more dreadfully shameful state. It lit up the room, but barely. I turned the light on, and it fell to the floor. I told you that it was in a dreadfully shameful state. It fell to the floor! I just walked into the room and broke a lightbulb. Luckily, it was still lluminated. It still lit up the entire room, but still very much barely so. I stepped forth and looked around.

The meta closet was larger than the regular closet. It was also dustier. In the middle of the barren, deserted room, was a simple beige sack, tied up with cheap golden rope that was poorly cut. I went over to the bag, and me being the curious son of a disrespectful adult I was, I opened that sack. The knot took me quite a while to get undone.

Once I undid the impossible knot, I peeked inside the bag. There was money! Los of it! All CAD. Why was it here? Maybe it was all of the store's saved up money to buy more stock. If so, that is a horrible place to keep it. I would recommend keeping a giant sack of Canadian money that just so happens to be all of the store's savings in literally any other place you could find. Even the bathrooms! Anyone brave enough to use a convenience store bathroom deserved a large excess of Canadian currency hidden in a sack.

Maybe, just to show how irresponsible it was, I took the giant bag of cash. Maybe, it was because I had said that I needed to come into contact with a large amount of money quickly. Maybe, I did not. Maybe, I am still deciding. In the meantime, I have an enormous sack of Canadian currency lying atop the never-washed floors of a convenience store, right behind the register.

Should I take it? I need money. But, so do the people who own the actual convenience store. That crispy-haired man needed some source of income or revenue. I couldn't do that to Mr. Crispy Hair Man. He was quite the respectable person, you know having his own business and all of that show. I couldn't take the money, well *I COULD,* but it would not be the right thing to do. I just couldn't do that to my poor manager. Also, y'know, he would definitely find out, and I would be fired faster than I could say the word pickles.

I did not want to be fired, as I would lose my steady income, but I would have a large amount of newfound cash. BUT, that cash would probably be in Mr. Crispy's hands, as it would be illegal for me not to hand it over. It would be illegal for me to take the giant sack of Canadian currency that was left in the middle of a meta closet home with me anyways!

I am decided. I will not take the money. Will NOT. NOT. I am sorry about the use of fragments. I will be taunted for the next couple of hours by the giant sack of Canadian money that is plopped right in front of my face. The money is daunting me, begging me to take it.

I will not listen.
Or at least I do not think I will.

Good loot today. Seventy-four dollars and fifty-three cents more. That is exactly seventy-four dollars and fifty-three cents more that goes into ny funds. After the announcement of the ATM, my funds are currently zero lollars out of twenty-eight-hundred and thirty-six AND fifty-three cents. That is just about zero percent. I might have to recalculate that, however, so lo not take my word for that.

I did not take the money! YAY! I have a small amount of willpower! Hurrah! I am a decent and capable human being. I have to stop writing. Family meeting, whatever that means.

I am writing from memory, so the conversation may not be exactly right.

"Is everyone here?" my mother asked impatiently.

Dallas counted. "All fifteen."

Sydney recounted. "Yep. All fifteen."

Jackson looked perturbed by the family meeting, as if it was interrupting his very, very busy schedule. "Why are we here?"

"It is a family meeting," my mother said triumphantly.

"What's that?" my sister Cynthia inquired.

"It is a meeting where we discuss very important family events," my mother politely responded.

"We've never had one of these before," Keith commented.

"Indeed, this is oddly new. Has father died again?" Kevin followed up.

"No, he is not dead times two, now just listen to mom," Miranda harshly scolded.

"Is everyone listening?" my mother asked angrily.

"Yes," everyone groaned, even me.

"We have the budget to go on a family trip. Where would you guys like to go? It is all your choice."

"Dallas, Texas!" Dallas shouted.

"Jackson, Mississippi!" Jackson screeched.

"Sydney, Australia!" Sydney suggested.

"Georgia! The state or the country!" Cynthia added.

"Belfast, in Britain!" Johnson continued.

"Tuvalu!" I chimed in, hoping it would work.

Everyone turned to me, Elisa scoffed, "Tuvalu ISN'T a place." I was too tired to argue.

The suggestions carried on, "Wellington, New Zealand!" Eliza started.

"Darwin, Australia," Elisa continued.

"Cleveland, Ohio!" Tim suggested.

"Angelo!" Keith added.

"Anchorage!" Kevin added.

"Tucson," Sammy quietly said.

"Istanbul!" May shouted with all of the strength of her respiratory system.

Our mother motioned for us to be quiet, "We do not have the budget to go out of the United States. In order to determine where we are going, we will have a vote. You can not vote more than once. We will go to a major city, or some city above that ranking. That is because those are the only ones that have airports. Obviously, we will not be going anywhere in state, so that rules out Minneapolis and St. Paul."

Everyone nodded, and my mother carried forth, "Everyone calm down and get ready."

"All of those who want to go to Boise may raise their hands."

No one raised their hands, "All of those who want to go to Denver may raise their hands."

Miranda and Sammy raised their hands, "That is two votes for Denver, Colorado. The Mile High City. All of those who want to go to Reno may raise their hands."

No one raised their hands, "All of those who want to go to Angelo may raise their hands."

Sally, Keith, and Tim shot their hands up, followed by the hand of Sydney, "That is four votes for Angelo. All of those who want to go to Tucson may raise their hands."

No one raised their hands. "All of those who want to go to Dallas may raise their hands."

Dallas and Cynthia's hand shot up. "Two votes for Dallas. All of those who want to go to Austin may raise their hands."

I raised my lone hand up, "One vote for Austin. All of those who want to go to Jackson may raise their hands."

Jackson, Johnson, Eliza, and Elisa raised their hands. "Four votes for Jackson. All of those who want to go to Toledo may raise their hands."

No one raised their hand, "OK. All of those who want to go to Cleveland may raise their hands."

Sydney and May raised their hands. "That is two votes. Two votes for Cleveland. All of those who want to go to Anchorage may raise their hands."

Kevin raised his lone hand, "That settles the last vote. The two places that tied are Jackson and Angelo. All of those who want to go to Angelo may raise their hands now."

Sydney, Keith, Kevin, Dallas, Elisa, and Eliza raised their hands. I interrupted the vote, "I think some people voted more than once on the first vote."

"That no longer is a concern that happens to be of a concern to me or concerning me in any way at all. Let us continue. It looks as though we are taking our family trip to Jackson, Mississippi!"

All fourteen of my siblings cheered, while I sat there, silent, not knowing what to think any more.

Jackson, Mississippi. Over one-thousand miles away from what I unfortunately call home. The drive would most likely take over nine hours, that is, if we do not fly there. If we flew, the flight would take about five whole hours, give or take twenty minutes. Either way, that is a lot of time to spend alone with my family. A LOT of time. Oh well, at least Jackson has an ATM.

Also, Jackson has an airport. Also, flights in Jackson might be cheaper. I will definitely have to check the flight prices from Jackson, Mississippi to Funafuti, Tuvalu once I am at the airport. They will probably be lower, since Jackson has a lower population.

Another benefit is that it is easier to escape from your family in an unknown city. There will be less surveillance by my family, as we are in a different city. I now have the perfect plan, I will escape the horrid city of Jackson, Mississippi and buy a flight all the way to Tuvalu.

Chapter Twelve

Sarajevo is a fun city; do not get me wrong. Sarajevo is a great city. It is NOT a great city when you are stuck in the airport for nine days straight. The next flight scheduled to Funafuti, Tuvalu, from Sarajevo, Bosnia is exactly nine days. That is nine days being alone in an airport. Nine days with nothing to do. I will have to live off of stuff that I bought on my shopping spree.

I ate one third of my food supply already in a series of stress-eating related incidents. That was enjoyable, yet very improper. Although I am dressed as a peasant off of the poor streets of rural Istanbul, I must not act like one of them! I composed myself. It has been four hours since the conversation with the attendant, and I am very worried about what I am going to do.

Where will I live? What will I do in my spare time? What will I say to those who are passing by and looking at me with a mix of disgust and appalment on their faces as they see me camped out in an airport like a common Greek vagrant. Perhaps I shall live on one of the benches in the store section. However, workers constantly go through that area, and I would be noticed in a matter of no time. Meanwhile, if I went and settled myself in the boarding area, I could wake up early enough to escape oncoming passerbyers.

I am decided. I will live inside of an airport in the boarding section and settle myself there for nine days. Great. Just great. Look at me, I am now even writing like a common vagrant. One thing is for certain, if I am to continue to live in this airport, I must continue my vagrant behavior and ways so that nobody will ever even think of me being a Neo-Ottoman heir.

I am settled in the boarding area. It turns out that each section of the airport is filled with maps! Filled. It's absolutely and undoubtedly wondrous. Past, present, and one odd-looking future predicting map.

In one room, there are only maps of Amsterdam. Amsterdam of all cities! It was quite the random choice. Alas, that is where I have set up camp. In the center of the room is the future predicting map. It is to the right of a present map, and to the left of a past map. Apparently, it is predicted that every single neighborhood in the city of Amsterdam will be made into superblocks. That map was made in 2020. The map is set in 2089. Wow, well that is just wrong. Amsterdam has been entirely decimated by the British nuclear weapons in the nuclear fallout of 2027. Amsterdam looked even more different in the past, it was quite a colonial city back in the day.

It is enjoyable waking up to those maps every morning, or at least I think. It was enjoyable to look at the first time. Past, present, and future maps of Amsterdam hung against the wall, seen every morning by someone who lived in the airport, and they would cheer her up every morning.

Also, there is a Dutch flag in the room. It is hanging from the boarding entrance above the tunnel used to enter the plane. It seems that the

141

entire room has a Dutch theme. I wonder if other rooms have country themes.

So, as it turns out, other rooms have themes as well. Right across the hall from my temporary living space is an Egypt themed room. That is quite the treat to see. There are maps everywhere. The chronology of the maps goes from left to right. From the Ancient Egyptian civilization settled along the Nile River to future predictions of Egypt. This time, the futuristic predictions were right. I think, in 2025, when the future map of Egypt was made, it was a political statement about Egypt. No matter the circumstances, the map was right. Egypt was depicted in 2090 as a desolate wasteland with not a single city left that bordered a Neo-Ottoman State. There are no current maps of Egypt, as it is a desert with no one living in it.

Hanging from the entrance are three flags, the Ancient Egyptian flag, the country of Egypt's flag when it was first established, and the updated flag of the Egyptian Republic. In all, I like the original flag of the Egyptian republic the best. Vexillology could amuse me all day, and it did. I spent all or most of my day traveling between rooms, looking at the different themes.

The next room had an American theme. America, such as foreign place. Lower standards for everything and no discernable social structure or classification. It is quite the laughable country, whereas Bosnia is quite the audable country. All across the walls were maps, from 1776 to 2090. It is quite amazing how America has developed as a country.

First, they were first actual country to gain independence. Then, manifest destiny got manifested into all of those colonialist crazed lunatics' heads and they expanded, a LOT. The Mexican-American War was quite the defeat, and it earned the US two new states, California and Texas, yet, the war is lost, like many others, in the spaces between the lines of history books. Then Hawaii and Alaska were colonized, as if the country wasn't already big enough. Then, there was an awkward phase where an excessively rich reality show host somehow became the freaking president of the United States. Who would ever vote for him?

After that, there was the Russian Economic collapse in 2021. Literally every single person in America cheered, unaware of the oncoming Taiwanese war. The Taiwanese-American War was a war that messed the economy of America up big-time. Then, Alaska followed the course of many other countries at the time and seceded. Then they subsequently found themselves in the Alaskan-Canadian War, which started over a border skirmish. Alaska was incorporated into Canada as the American government watched slyly. The Greenland Wars were an interesting time for America. They actually fought ON the same side as Canada. Then, in 2048, the Neo-Soviet Empire reformed in all of its glory.

The American government went from being slap happy over Alaska to internally screaming over the Neo-Soviet Empire. It was the return of America's worst enemy in history. Of course, when the Warsaw Incident happened, America was more than glad to help interfere and spread an infection. Then, after they thought all of the worst was over, Taiwan started expanding. Taiwan started expanding rapidly, very rapidly. Soon, Taiwan grew close to bigger than America itself. America went crazy and puppeted the government of Canada for tens of millions of dollars. In 2055, the Icelandic Wars started, and Alaska was involved.

It was America versus Britain again, but this time, they were battling over Iceland. America was close, as Greenland had been incorporated into the Alaskan territory after the Greenland Wars, but was still part of Canada. So now, Alaska, a.k.a. America (including the relatively new Greenland territories) was fighting a war against Britain over Iceland. Talk about drama. Alas, the Icelandic Wars did not last long, for the Alaskan victory occurred in 2057.

Everything was peaceful in North America until a fatefully horrible day in 2072. The North American Political Fallout had started. Canada (which was still part of America) versus America versus the Central American Alliance. Whilst this was happening, the Taiwanese Dynasty had finished their expansion, as they now spanned over more than ninety-nine percent of the continent of Asia. The day had come in which Taiwan was larger than America. Still in the midst of this decades long war, the Arctic Wars came upon the horizon. It was America versus northeastern Canadian territories (which were still a part of America) versus Britain versus Icelandic forces versus the Taiwanese Dynasty. It was all of these empires fighting over the Arctic. The Arctic War has yet to end, although it is impossible to say who will win at this point in time. Finally, in 2082, the North American Political Fallout came to a long needed end. America had won and now controls all of the mainland continent of North America.

I do not know what lies in America's future, but no matter what, it will be very interesting.

The room after the American room was a Turkish themed room. Again, from left to right, it was maps of the past leading up to the present. Turkey's history is way too complicated to even start to explain in my journal. That means that I shall not. I noticed something out of the corner of my eye. There were newspapers! I had not noticed these before. There must have also been some in the American themed room, but not the Egyptian themed room because Egypt is a desolate wasteland at this point, and not in the Dutch themed room, for the Netherlands is now a part of Germany.

I pulled out the newspapers. There were newspapers from two days. The headlines surprised me, enthralled me, and scared me. The first headline read: *Taiwanese-Ottoman Tie! India: A Country Divided*. I cut out the article nicely using scissors and pasted it into my notebook below.

Taiwanese-Ottoman Tie! India: A Country Divided

As of 10:17 this morning, the Taiwanese-Ottoman War has come to an end. The Taiwanese-Ottoman War began in 2081. It has been eleven years since the start of this bloody and horrific war, and it is finally finished with a decisive victory by no one. Bad news for both the residents of the

Taiwanese Dynasty and the New Greek Empire, as neither side has won. On a side note, although the war is officially called the Taiwanese-Ottoman War, the New Greek Empire conquered the Neo-Ottoman Empire before they could win the war. The New Greek Empire created a treaty to stop the war from damaging their newfound economy.

India was the start of the war, and India was the end of the war. The New Greek government and the Taiwanese Dynasty have created the Indian Division Treaty of 2092 and it was signed 10:17 this morning in Nagpur, which is the city in the exact center of India. Antonis Melis and Lin Godinez met in Nagpur yesterday night and signed the treaty this morning. India has been split exactly in half. With all Indian land east of Nagpur now being Taiwanese, and all land west being Greek. Nagpur as a city has even been divided, where a united community once stood confidently, a divided nation's heart has fallen. The New Greek Empire will keep the territories of Pakistan, Afghanistan, and Turkmenistan. The Taiwanese Dynasty will retain control of their territories of Uzbekistan, Tajikistan, Kyrgyzstan, and Kazakhstan. Nepal, Bhutan, and Bangladesh will revert to Taiwanese control, whilst the island of Ceylon will be given to the New Greek Empire.

The country of India has been divided before in the colonial ages, but now, it is a nation split down the middle, with two major world powers on the sides. Analysts say that languages such as Hindi Turkish and Turkish Urdu will be redeveloped under Taiwanese control and influence. Other things such as currency and culture will change. India has never been a country for using only one currency, yet with the Taiwanese Dynasty taking

146

over the east, it will be impossible to stay away from that. The culture of India has changed through every single one of its colonizations. Analysts say that the culture may change so drastically from east to west that it will seem like two countries.

After the conquest of the Neo-Ottoman Empire, the New Greek Empire strived to stop most of the current conflicts. It is most likely because of the New Greek Empire's lack of a proper military. The Ukrainian Confederacy has put up more than enough offers to end the war over southern Ukraine and Crimea, yet all of the offers involve giving up territory, something that was fundamentally against the beliefs in the Neo-Ottoman government. With the New Greek Empire, they are looking towards ceding Crimea, and have been given a grace period to remove their soldiers from the battle fronts in southern Ukraine and Crimea. Despite initially being allies, the Serbian rebels are still rebelling against the New Greek Empire. The New Greek Empire has plans to initiate a test-period in which Serbia will be freed from Greek rule, but if the government does something the New Greek Empire deems "wrong," Serbia will be put back into the hands of the New Greek Empire. Of course, Serbian rebels do not enjoy this plan. The Mecca front is one that has not yet been considered. The Mecca front is such a recent conflict that the New Greek Empire may not be willing to give it up. Only time will tell which the new semi-functional government.

I pasted the next article below. The headline caught me by such surprise that my heart seemed to stop for a second. This article was from today.

The Neo-Ottoman Heir has escaped captivity

Only a short while ago, a Georgian refugee known as Gennadiya Petrov was admitted into the Istanbul Prison. A day before that, Dimos Vassallos was killed after a very controversial speech. Gennadiya Petrov was the one who pulled the trigger. That was less than a week after the Neo-Ottoman heir to the throne, Maurie Osman was "killed" by Greek rebellion forces. After a DNA test was done on Gennadiya Petrov, it was found that she was actually Maurie Osman. Maurie Osman shot the ruler of the New Greek Empire and was admitted into the Istanbul Prison. Maurie had made up an identity for herself, or she had gone insane. She was later put in solitary after she was found with a gun. Yesterday, her solitary cell was found empty with a knife in it. The cell bars had been cut. The guard no longer had his key ring. It would seem that Gennadiya Petrov, or should I say, Maurie Osman has broken out of the Istanbul Prison.

Maurie Osman's knife was later identified to be a pineapple knife. When guards in the prison run out of food for those in solitary, they have been known to give prisoners pineapples and a knife to cut them. Apparently, no one has attempted to use a pineapple knife to break out of prison. Guards have gotten the knife back forcibly before they could attempt o escape using it. The guard on duty, known as Shegan, had forgotten to ake the knife back. Shegan was promptly fired.

The whereabouts of Maurie Osman are unknown. It is suspected she s checked into a hotel near the city center known as the Osman Royal lotel. The irony is the least of the police's concerns. Her reservation was nade a while ago, and is void at this point. Police suspect that Maurie has ived there illegally since she got out of prison. A full investigation will be aunched tomorrow morning by local police forces. If anyone has any knowledge of the whereabouts or any other information regarding Maurie Osman that could be beneficial please contact your local police.

This article surprised me. I hope the taxi driver did not know who I am. I now need to be extra careful when it comes to social interactions with strangers. If someone even so much as suspects that I am, I will be hunted down and killed. That would be bad.

After I took a hot second to calm down, I went to the American room to see if they had newspapers. Perhaps the turmoil in America would help me cope with my own troubles.

I clipped out the front page article, and two that came after it. I just wanted to keep them in my journal for later. I think that they reflect current issues in America.

Brasilia Strikes Back! A New Trade War and a Developing Conflict

On Monday, the United States of America spun off a new round of tariffs against the government of Brazil, totaling over four and a half billion dollars in damage. These tariffs were instigated by Brazil's decreased amount of exports to the United States the Tuesday before the tariffs were instituted. This came from Brazil's struggling economic state, which has been on decline since the Brazilian Economic Collapse in 2039.The government has finally began to cut down on unnecessary exports to non-allied countries, such as the United States and the South Brazilian Free State. The excess amount of exports were not being met with sufficient imports as compensation, so Brazil cutting down on the excess will help them solidify trading relations with those who will compensate.

This morning at 3:22, the Brazilian government struck back. To get straight to the point, the damage is over nine and a half billion dollars. The United States may not see this as a threat, but the specific tariffs addressed products such as raw sugar, soybeans, and Poultry meat. These products are prominent Brazilian imports in America, and the economy of America is suspected to relapse from its all-time high and come close to collapsing if these tariffs continue. Brasilia stated that "If the tariffs are too continue, iron ore and crude petroleum will be taxed as well, if not, then we will pull back one billion dollars of tariffs at a time."

America's response came in the plan of a new round of tariffs. The damage? Only two billion dollars. Remember, this is only in the form of a plan. If this plan carries out, Brasilia will hit America back harder than the American economy can handle.

Analysts say that Brazil and America are headed for a trade war. Along with America and Brazil being enemies, the tariffs will draw the government against each other. Along with a trade war, an actual military conflict may arise.

Arctic War Drawn Out After America's loss of Reykjavik

The United States of America is in the midst of a war with Canadian rebels, Britain, Iceland, and the Taiwanese Dynasty in and over the Arctic Circle. Canadian rebels and Icelandic forces are part of a forced alliance, both wanting freedom from their colonial owners. Britain and the United States are in an unlikely alliance for once, both wanting equal control over the Arctic, mainly Iceland (for Britain) and northern Siberia (for the United States of America). Meanwhile, the Taiwanese Dynasty is trying to keep control of Siberia.

The United States currently owns Alaska, Northern Canada, and Greenland. Britain owns a handful of coastal cities such as Vik in Iceland. Canadian rebels own some rebelling cities in Nunavut. The Taiwanese

Dynasty owns all of Siberia and northern Russia. Iceland owns the majority of Iceland still. Besides the Arctic War, the Alaskan-Taiwanese War is going on. The Alaskan-Taiwanese War is part of the Arctic War, yet is the most prolonged battle, and has been going on for two years.

Yesterday, at 9:38 at night, the United State lost control of the city of Reykjavik, which was its last foothold in Iceland. Iceland's capital had been owned by American forces since the beginning of the Arctic War in 2082. It was the first invasion in the Arctic War. Reykjavik was the most important city in the Arctic War, as the Icelandic government and their organized rebellion was destroyed as soon as Reykjavik was taken over. Now that the Icelandic rebellion has reconquered Reykjavik, they will soon rise and most likely take over all the rest of Iceland.

Since Reykjavik is back where it was originally, the entirety of the Arctic War is basically reset. The conflicts that had happened in the start of the war will occur again. The entire war will be drawn out and the conflicts will restart. The Arctic War will last longer than expected.

Bosnian Convertible Mark Being Considered for New Currency in America

The Bosnian Convertible Mark is being considered as a new currency to be used in the United States. There is a list of currencies being considered to be a new currency used in the United States of America. This ist will be given to state governments, who will then choose which new currencies or currency to adopt. Other currencies being considered for the list are the Swiss Franc, the Cayman Islands Dollar, Panamanian Balboa, and the Cuban peso.

The Cuban Peso, the Panamanian Balboa, the Cayman Islands Dollar, and the Swiss Franc are all currencies with a one to one exchange rate to USD. Meanwhile, the Bosnian Convertible Mark has an exchange rate that is not even close to one to one.

The Bosnian Convertible Mark is being considered for a very different reason. The Bosnian Convertible Mark's value has been soaring past expectations. In one single day, the Bosnian Convertible Mark's value increased by three point two percent! That is a record high increase in Bosnian history. Because of the newfound value, investing in Bosnian Convertible Mark, and then withdrawing stocks after its value skyrockets again could be quite beneficial to the American economy and to the American population.

The American government is expected to choose the Bosnian Convertible Mark. Vincent Kugler commented on the matter: "The choice of the Bosnian Convertible Mark is in the interest of the people. With the ability to invest in the Bosnian Convertible Mark, personal finances will improve. Do not dismiss this opportunity. This opportunity will not come again."

I went to the next themed room. It was French themed. I enjoyed the flags and the history, but the newspapers caught my eye. I will end this entry with one last article. Overall, it was a good day. Even if I did spend it looking at flags and reading newspapers.

The Isle Of Man? A Secluded Paradise, But Not for Much Longer

The Isle Of Man is a tiny country in the middle of the Irish Sea. With its own capital (Douglas), currency (Manx Pound), government (absolute monarchy), and culture. This island paradise has been secluded from the world for the past seventy years or so. The last mention of any colonial owner was in the form of a worn-out Union Jack flown in Port Erin. Because of this, it is suspected that the Isle Of Man used to be part of the British Empire. Despite Britain owning the islands that surround it, they have no wishes to recolonize it. John Philips, the president of Britain, made an official comment last Sunday:

"The Isle Of Man has always been a secluded island. Even when it was owned by a colonial ruler, it did not abide by the rules. The Isle Of Man ignored the colonial government that was established, and created their own. Britain, as a country with proper fundamentals, has no interest in taking over this country."

Meanwhile, French forces are already deployed and on their way to the Isle Of Man. They were sent off on Sunday, after John Philips said that

Britain would not take over the isle. The French army is currently involved in a (so far) successful raid and conquest of the Isle Of Man. The French president, Ludovic Boudet, made an official comment on Monday at a press conference:

"John Philips may not want a paradise, but I want any proper territory I can get. Although it may be paradise simply because of its seclusion, it must abide to the rules of society. If we did not invade, then someone would have."

The raid has gone as far north as the city of Ramsey, and the French army only has three more small towns to go. There is no way that this tropical, secluded, paradise will survive for much longer.

That was too bad. The Isle Of Man sounds like it could have been a perfect paradise to escape to. Alas, the country has been taken over by France. It is no Tuvalu anymore.

Chapter Thirteen

Planes are NOT fun. Especially for five hours. Five hours of being in a metal tube that was flung through the sky. Seats have gotten smaller, yet flights have gotten longer. So, I am cramped in a "miniature" plane seat for three and a half more hours. I am next to Dallas, Kevin, and Keith. The three idiots of the family and me. Why did I think this would be fun?

At least it would not be a nine hour drive in the backseat of a car that smelled like fish carcasses. On a plane ride, I was able to get up and walk around the cabin. Also, I was able to get service and meal tubes or snack tubes. It seems like the plane ride would have been much better than the car ride. I was in the window seat, meaning that every single time that I wanted to get out of my seat, I had to tediously scooch past my buffoon brothers.

I got up at one point and when I came back, the buffoon by the name of Dallas had scarfed down my meal tube. That was quite fun. I can not wait for this excessively long plane ride to be over.

It has been an hour since I last wrote. I found a nice article on Jackson, Mississippi in the back pocket. I cut out the article and pasted it in here. I think that when I look back at this journal, I will enjoy seeing what the quaint city of Jackson, Mississippi looked like in 2092.

Welcome to the City of Jackson, Mississippi

The city of Jackson, Mississippi is a major city in The United States of America with a population of seven-hundred-ninety-thousand-eighty-four. It is a city of tourists, and it is built for that. With hotels, stores, many attractions, and an airport, it is the perfect tourist destination.

The many tourist destinations and attractions are well known across the world. They have a large interactive library museum. It is the only library museum that allows you to enjoy the books in the library museum. Although the selection in the library is not as extensive as most library museums, it is quite interesting to the average tourist in Jackson. The large interactive museum is located on three-hundred North State Street.

There is also the Museum of Mississippi History, located on Two-twenty-two North State Street. The museum showcases the history of Mississippi, when it first became a state, through the civil war, through the political fallout, and through modern times.

Finally, there is a dormant volcano called the Jackson Volcano under the abandoned coliseum on 1207 Mississippi Street. It has been turned into a museum on the surface, and is entirely open to visitors. For a more extensive tour, there are elevators that go as far down as is safe in the Jackson Volcano.

When visiting Jackson, Mississippi, there are some things you may want to know. The languages spoken in Jackson, Mississippi are French, English, and certain types of French creole. The currencies used in Mississippi are USD, CAD, BBD, and BSD. The most commonly accepted currency is USD. Things in Jackson are quite cheap compared to other major cities. Such as a map, which is three dollars and eighty cents in Jackson, whilst it is five dollars and ninety-nine cents in Angelo.

We here at Mississippi East Airlines hope you enjoy Jackson, Mississippi, and we hope you enjoy your flight.

Reading the article made me more optimistic about visiting the quaint city of Jackson, Mississippi. Maybe, just maybe, not certainly, the five hour flight with three buffoons will be worth it.

I was wrong. I was very, very wrong. I was so very wrong. Goodness gracious was I wrong. I am hiding in the airplane's bathroom stall and I am writing in this journal. Those buffoons that wrongly go by the HUMAN names of Kevin, Keith, and Dallas are inhumane and soul-depriving once they even start to vibrate their mouths to make human sounding noises known as conversation. In the name of the depressingly gloomy state of Minnesota, why, oh why, do I have to live with those apes? Have they not fully evolved yet?

I have been hiding in this stall for twenty-nine minutes and I swear to whatever freaking god the Hmong peoples who live in Minnesota believe in, they will only drag me out if I am a lifeless corpse or the plane has landed. The knocking and pounding on the doors would NOT persuade me.

will stay here as long as I need to. Those flight attendants can drag me out by my cold dead hands!

The bathroom stall is very comfortable, roomy, cozy, and overall homey. I can stretch my legs A L L the way out, and I actually have enough room to breathe. I s t r e t c h e d my legs out across the room and relaxed. I was finally safe, despite the angry mob forming a line in front of the stall door.

It has been an hour!!!! There is only one hour left. The crowds have gone away and left me to curl up and sleep. I feel like a sloth. I have a couple of in-flight magazines that I have read through dozens of times on end. I will spend my time clipping them out so you can read them. Ah, the refreshing, yet eloquent art of free in-flight magazine articles. I picked a few about news, and I have shared them in my journal. Hopefully, these will be of use to me sometime later in my life as something to look back on.

The Mecca Front: an American Intervention Waiting to Happen

After the conquest of the Neo-Ottoman Empire by Greek rebels, the president, Antonis Melis, promised that he would put an end to conflicts within and around the New Greek Empire. For the most part, he has fulfilled this promise. The Taiwanese-Ottoman War has finally come to an end, after eleven years of the bloody war. The Ukrainian Confederacy has given the New Greek Empire a grace period to remove soldiers from Crimea and southern Ukraine. In the western outskirts of the New Greek Empire, an agreement has been proposed to Serbian rebels to end the fighting. However, along the southern outskirts of the New Greek Empire, a conflict is as much of a war as when the Neo-Ottomans were fighting it.

After conquering Riyadh, the Mecca Front arose. It was the Neo-Ottoman Empire against the Saudi Territories over the capital of the Islamic faith. The Neo-Ottoman Empire, wanting to prove itself as a true Islamic country, had never given up the Mecca Front. The New Greek Empire has followed in their footsteps. Antonis Melis was asked about this matter in a press conference on Friday. He then commented the following statement:

"The Neo-Ottoman Empire was never truly Islamic. If it is allowed for them to still want the Islamic capital, why can't the New Greek Empire want it as well? We rule the same areas, meaning they have the same Islamic population. With the takeover of the capital of an entire faith, maybe more governments and populations internationally will start to see the New Greek Empire properly."

It appears that Antonis Melis's attempts at peacemaking have come to an abrupt halt at the end of the Riyadh territories. The United States of America, looking for a new ally to replace the Neo-Ottoman Empire, regarded Antonis Melis's peacemaking as a good sign for their relations future. Now that they have continued the Mecca Front, the front in the empire America was most worried over, America is looking to intervene. At a press conference yesterday morning, the president of the United States of America, Shawn Conover, brought up the Mecca Front to the reporters' surprise. He promptly commented the following statements:

"The Mecca Front is a front that shall not be disregarded. If Antonis Melis truly wants to end their conflicts, then they wouldn't hold onto their last strand of hope they have with the Mecca Front. The city of Mecca should not belong to any one country or empire, but to the world as a private territory, as it was before. If the Mecca Front continues, a military intervention may be required immediately. We can not and shall not let the entirety of the Islamic faith belong to one country's hands. If Antonis Melis continues on like this, action will be taken."

Details on the military intervention have surfaced. The American government is prepared to send out over one million soldiers to Mecca to guard the city. The plans involve surrounding the city and holding the positions for days, or weeks, or months, until Mecca is reestablished as an international territory. Only time will tell if this intervention will be necessary.

The Tribes Rebranding as Countries in Scandinavia

While you may not know it, an old map of Scandinavia was simple. There was Norway, Sweden, Denmark, and Iceland. These countries constantly fought, but eventually collapsed in 2079 after the spread of the Norwegian Plague, the populations collapsed. Currently, there are about forty-seven Norwegian kingdoms and confederacies, fourteen Danish confederacies, eight Icelandic tribes, and around eleven Swedish states. The most infamous of these states, tribes, kingdoms, and confederacies is Upper Gotland, an authoritative Swedish state.

Recently, the Kingdom of Bosnia has been importing large amounts of scrap metal to Scandinavian tribes. They have imported it to twenty-one Norwegian tribes and three Swedish states, including Upper Gotland. Other Norwegian tribes have looked in to these investments as well.

These newfound riches have transformed many tribes into countries. Upper Gotland has recently conquered all of the island of Gotland using their new imports. Norwegian tribes such as the Finmark tribe have started to rebrand themselves as countries. The Finmark tribe has introduced a new system of government and social classes, like other Norwegian tribes. The tribe in Hœrlend is combining with nearby tribes to further establish a proper government.

In Denmark, a meeting of all fourteen documented tribes is being called in Copenhagen, a city currently owned by the Swedish leading tribe in the area, the Hæland tribe. The Hæland tribe has given permission to the Danish tribes to hold the meeting. The Danish tribes will divide up what is left of Denmark into three tribes. This will require days of negotiation and border division. The meeting will be held tomorrow afternoon.

In Iceland, the Arctic War has blown apart the seemingly inseparable country of Iceland. Where there used to be major Icelandic tribes, British forces or American forces have taken the cities that held the tribes together. Recently, the Blue Lagoon tribe has retaken the Icelandic capital city of Reykjavik. Although it may seem that these tribes are fighting to reform the country of Iceland, they are all fighting against one another. As soon as the Blue Lagoon tribe took over Reykjavik, the Grindavik tribe fought against the Blue Lagoon tribe.

Overall, now is not a time for tranquility in Scandinavia. Empires and tribes are pitched against each other once again, and new countries will form where Norway, Sweden, Denmark, and Iceland once stood. Where divided countries fell, new tribes will rise and reconquer Scandinavia. Only time will tell what will happen in the depths of Scandinavia.

Five Upcoming Major Cities in the United States

There are thirteen major cities left in the United States, however some cities are starting to catch up to them. In order to be the lowest tier of a major city, a city has to have a population of seven-hundred-seventy-thousand peoples. To go with this, the city has to have the means to withstand the population and a proper government. In the public's eyes, it is only the people's opinion that determines what is and is not a major city. So, The Jackson Times has rounded up five cities that have the potentials to be major cities.

163

Detroit, Michigan

Detroit is not the capital of the state of Michigan, yet it has a reasonably large population of five-hundred and one thousand. The reason this is on the list is because of its major population growth curves. Detroit as a city was left behind and abandoned in 2028, a year after the nuclear fallout. The citizens did not believe that Michigan would be spared. Also, tensions with nearby Canada were insanely high at the time. Since populations have migrated back from Toledo and Cleveland, the population growth rate has reached fourteen point one percent in the last year. That is the highest rate recorded in the Midwest in seventy years! Soon, Detroit will grow to have a population that makes them a major city.

Portland, Maine

Portland, Maine is a city on the rise. Although the population growth is less than steady, the state government of Maine is working on prioritizing Portland, Maine as a major city. Instead of focusing on the capital, which most state governments do, Maine as a state has focused on Portland instead. Portland has always been a popular city in the eyes of the public, and it continues to be. It is even a popular vacation spot. Portland has been given many privileges by the state government of Maine that other cities could only dream of getting. Portland has its own airport, despite not being a major city. It is one of the only cities globally to have one without being a major city. To add to this, Maine has focused marketing campaigns and ads round the city of Portland. Although the population is less than adequate, the city of Portland, Maine is on the rise.

Portland, Oregon

Portland, Oregon is a city that is economically developing faster than even major cities are. Oregon has poured almost all of the Oregon state government's budget into developing the city economically. Again, like the state government of Maine, the state government of Maine has not focused on the state capital, but rather an admirable city in the public's eyes. The population of Portland, Oregon is just about four-hundred-thirty-one-thousand. This less than ideal population does not help Portland, Oregon's case for being a major city. Meanwhile, the GDP is soaring past expectations. The GDP growth rate over the past year has reached seventeen percent! This excessive growth is contributing to Portland, Oregon's case as a major city. Hopefully, the GDP growth will influence the population growth.

Houston, Texas

The state of Texas has already been given the privilege of having two different major cities with large populations and economies, yet Houston is an up and coming city. Surprisingly, the formerly-very-popular Houston is not one of them. The cities of Austin and Dallas are already major cities, and they are both in the state of Texas. Texas's population as a state is so large that it can be spread between many major cities. Houston's

165

population has reached seven-hundred-thousand as of December 2091, and the population is expected to steadily grow and reach major city tier status by May, 2092. It is possible that it could reach the proper population rank earlier, especially if the GDP growth increases, as more people will migrate towards Houston.

San Francisco, California

In 2027, after the nuclear fallout destroyed the city of Angelo (Los Angeles) and the residents of San Francisco thought that they were next. It only made sense, however the city of San Francisco survived, but without its three million people. San Franciscans moved back to California once the fallout blew over, but not to San Francisco. There was a California initiative program to reestablish the proper population of Los Angeles that included a law that one who moved to Los Angeles from another state would have half of their rent paid by the state. Whilst the initiative cost millions upon millions, it restored Los Angeles's population and reestablished the city as Angelo. Other cities such as Sacramento and San Diego were ignored, just like San Francisco. The difference is that San Francisco's population has started to migrate back from Los Angeles. While this may mean that Angelo's population is shrinking, San Francisco's population is gradually increasing.

Overall, the writers here at The Jackson Times all agree that there is only one of these cities that can truly say they are the next major city.

Detroit, Michigan is a city that's population growth has reached fourteen point one percent. Detroit may not be a favorite for tourists, and may not have a large population to grow off of, but Detroit is expected to be the next major city. Although many people may not like this fact, it is the truth.

These newspapers were very interesting in my opinion. In my opinion, Houston, Texas should have been picked over Detroit, Michigan and over the others. Of course I was partial to my home state. I can not wait to get off of this airplane.

There are thirty minutes left in my flight. The flight attendants have come back, angrier than before. They had a key. They busted me out of the bathroom. Flight attendants just forcibly removed me from an airplane bathroom. That was a fun addition to my already miserable trip. When I got back, my brother by the name of Dallas had scarfed down another one of my snack tubes. I can not wait for this flight to finally be over.

It has been twenty-nine minutes. The pilot just came on the speaker.

"I am very sorry folks, it looks like we are not set to land because of scheduling errors, so we will be circling around for the next twenty to forty minutes. Again, I am sorry for the delay. No missed connections can be refunded."

I can not wait to finally land in Jackson, Mississippi.

Chapter Fourteen

Sarajevo is great, except for the fact that I can not get out of this airport, as I would be spotted and killed. I have gotten a job. I have also gotten a complete makeover at a salon. Now, no one will ever spot me. Do not worry, the salon workers were either too dumb or too foreign to understand who I really was. One thought that "Surujevoo" was a country in the Balkans. Another was from Dublin, and understood negative three words that I said. That was fun, but more so entertaining. It turns out that the two I talked about were a couple. They suit each other well.

I got my hair styled and then went out and bought shaggy Soviet era coats. My hairstyle looks frizzy and unkempt, like Trotsky without hairspray as a girl. I am going for a Soviet/Russian theme. I am wearing an enormous fur Russian coat, sporting a frizzy mess of hair atop my head, and wearing gloves and boots that were fit for a Russian soldier from 2049. Overall, I look very **NOT**-Turkish and very **NOT**-Ottoman. I have been speaking in a horrible Russian accent since I got my makeover. It is almost like my Georgian accent, which I used when I pretended to be Gennadiya Petrov in prison, but deeper and more foreign.

I got up with my Russian lieutenant uniform and walked right on over to the nearest convenience store. After I had spent all of this money on the makeover, I needed to earn some money back. As is common knowledge, the only way to do that is to get a job or commit a felony. I have chosen to do the former of the options. I have been employed at the local airport convenience store, well, one of the local airport convenience stores.

I got the job immediately, because they were hiring and the manager did not care. My Russian/Soviet identity has been able to be believed so far by everyone I have interacted with. My name is Nozdryova Lisenka Kirillovna, not Maurie Osman, and not Gennadiya Petrov.

Apparently, Nozdryova Lisenka Kirillovna does not like to interact with others. My human interactions with people have gone horribly well. When people ask me what thing to buy, I point to something and say "Is good." I can not believe that that is the limit of my vocabulary. That is less vocabulary than I used as the miserable Georgian identity of Gennadiya Petrov. It is simply infuriating to use such little vocabulary when I, as a royal princess and proper heir to the throne to the Neo-Ottoman Empire or the New Greek Empire, have such a large and expansive vocabulary that can not be encompassed by the words: "is good."

It is demeaning and patronizing to act this way, and I can not wait for the day in the (somewhat) near future in which I can finally escape to the wondrous safehaven of Tuvalu. Meanwhile, I am being paid thirty-eight Turkish Liras per hour, which just so happens to be directly lower than minimum wage. It is also demeaning and patronizing to be paid directly lower than minimum wage. I can not wait for this to be over.

The convenience store I work at is right next to the salon run by the foreign woman and the stupidest assistant you could ever even imagine. It is one of the smaller convenience stores in this particular section of this airport

hat is vastly too large, yet that is a good thing, because it means that they
will have lower standards no matter what I do. However, this also means
that they pay me significantly less. Although it may seem like is a bad trade
off, it means that I am held to no standards. I am not held to a single
standard or bar in this insignificant store, which is not demeaning or
patronizing in that matter, as I can act however I would like to and do
whatever I would like to.

I do not get paid extra for how many sales I make, even if I make a
thousand more than expected, even if I make a million or a billion more
sales than is expected. However, that means that I can make as many or as
few sales as I want to. I can purposefully act like I do not work there when,
in the actual reality of this horrible world, I am too tired to talk to people
because I am trapped in this absolutely horrible airport.

I have had one encounter in which my real identity was almost
compromised. I was sitting at the checkout desk, reading the newspaper. Of
course, as expected, the value of the Bosnian Convertible Mark has gone
through the roof yet again, even though the Bosnian Kingdom is in the midst
of a war with its tinier and less armed counterpart, Bosnian Herzegovina.
Whilst I was reading the news, I was spotted by a young man, appearing to
be in his late twenties or early thirties, wearing a beanie with the Serbian
nationalist coat of arms, and a beat-up and worn-out gray (or maybe white
since it was worn down so much by use and wear and tear) jacket with green
cargo pants that looked like they were twenty or thirty years old and a nice

pair of military boots to accompany the rest of his off-putting outfit and to act as his proper footwear.

As this rather substantial man looked at me ominously, I ignored him. I could only think about he could get arrested by wearing a Serbian nationalist beanie in the heart and center, and the capital, of the Bosnian Kingdom with no context. He looked at me suspiciously, and then looked at a photo in his hands. He looked back and forth between me and the picture for what seemed as if it was forever before he finally set off to go into the store. Now, mind you, he was quite far away from the store, and was quite the slow walker. Or maybe he was walking slowly as to not draw attention to his violation of the law he was wearing a top and on his head proudly.

Once he started slowly and gradually towards the convenience store I was sitting at the checkout desk in, he was tackled down by airport security guards for the reason of possession of outside propaganda. He was arrested for wearing a Serbian nationalist beanie. The governments of any country will arrest anyone for anything. The man was tackled down and dragged away in front of my eyes.

It is normal to be arrested for propaganda. Even saying "Canada will rise again" or "The Swiss are the rightful owners of the Alps" can get you arrested in the United States of America and the Neo-French Empire respectively.

In the Neo-Ottoman Empire, the Bosnian Kingdom, and Bosnian Herzegovina, the rules are the strictest. Back when the Neo-Ottoman Empire used to exist (and I was the heir), someone could get arrested for even waving a Serbian flag. There was no *free speech*, there should never be *free speech*. One must not openly rebel against their own country or nationality. To rebel against one's country, empire, confederacy, kingdom, state, tribe, or even nationality is to rebel against oneself.

In the Bosnian Kingdom, it is not even allowed to talk about Bosnian history and politics in a negative light. To say: "The Bosnian Kingdom has an okay chance of winning the war against Bosnian Herzegovina, just not like, one-hundred percent" is to commit a crime. One must not have no belief in their country. For one to say that their country may not win a war or even a battle is to say that you do not believe in where you live, you do not believe that your surroundings, your nationality, can succeed. To a certain extent, it means that you do not believe you will ever even succeed. In Bosnian Herzegovina, the rules are the same. In most cases, it is illegal to talk about any politics or history regarding or concerning Bosnian Herzegovina or any historical counterpart. As it should be.

Meanwhile, in the lousy United States of America, there is *free speech*. *Free speech* is the low point of the human race. *Free speech* has never accomplished anything. *Free speech* allows people to burn the flags of their country. *Free speech* allows people to hate their country. *Free speech* means that you can do whatever you want, and it will be regarded as legal. I met someone from the United States of America once, in the humble city of Gebze. I was traveling for a boring business meeting with my father. He was at a local coffee shop, wearing a fez. I asked him where he was from. He

173

was from America. I then asked him why he moved. He said, and I quote: "The United States of America is a joke. It has a horrible economy. It has a corrupt government. It is an awful country." *Free speech* let him do that. *Free speech* let him hate his country. *Free speech* made him the horrible person he was. *Free speech* is the bane of this world's existence.

To show you just how effective NOT using *free speech* is, I will give you a couple of examples where *free speech* would have started a war. In 2066, a Serbian nationalist radical group infiltrated a soccer match in Albania. The match was between the national Serbian soccer team and the national Albanian soccer team. Albania was winning, three to one. It was an embarrassment for the usually good (or at least usually better than the Albanian national soccer team) national Serbian soccer team. The radical Serbian nationalist group known as Cvetkinist rebels threw a few bombs made of an alcoholic beverage set on fire through cloth. The stadium was decimated. Through the rubble and debris, Albanian police found one of the original vodka bottles. It said *Nema krsta bez tri prsta.* This means "There is no cross without three fingers," which is a reference to the infamous Serbian nationalist three-finger salute. It is meant to show that Serbians are the rightful orthodoxes, rather than Albanians. The members of the group expected to be involved were arrested, and the members of the group suspected NOT to be involved were arrested.

The next example happened in Laos (in the Sino-ASEAN organization during its decline) in 2053. This happened in the midst of the Sino-ASEAN political fallout. In the famously religious temple of Angkor

Wat, in the middle of the night, a Chinese nationalist spray painted the words 遵守规则, meaning "compliance by the rules." The infamous Chinese nationalist, Xuan Na, spray painted these words to make fun of Laos's disobedience when it came to converting the religion of all of the Sino-ASEAN organization. China had ruled that every country in the organization should switch to the religion in China, as China owned the entire Sino-ASEAN organization. Xuan Na agreed with this change, but the government of Laos did not. Xuan Na was arrested and detained in Laos until the day he died.

The final example is the harshest example of what would could have been allowed if *free speech* was allowed worldwide. In 2038, a Turkish (by birth origin) protester took down the Neo-Ottoman Empire's flag and replaced it with the flag of a nearby Greek nationalist rebellion radical group called Petrakists, who believed that the Greeks rightfully owned Istanbul, which he was a part of. The man went by the name of Thanasis Rigas. He replaced the Neo-Ottoman flag three and a half hours before the official meeting started. The flag was placed in a conference room where the Neo-Ottoman Empire was set to negotiate terms of ownership over all of the island of Cyprus, and the Greek nationalist rebellion radical group, of course, did not enjoy the fact that this conference meeting was even being held in the first place. The Neo-Ottoman flag was found at his house after he was arrested. However, he was not caught the first time he committed a crime. The second time involved fire. The second time involved Greek fire.

Over two years later, Thanasis Rigas struck the Neo-Ottoman Empire for the second and last time with an infamous act of vandalism and terrorism. As he belonged to the Greek nationalist radical rebellion group, and he himself was a Petrakist, he had access to many special forms of technology, including the ever fought-over formula for the infamously horrid Greek fire. Two hours before a conference meeting, another conference meeting with Greece about terms of Greek surrender, he set the flag on fire. This was the first documented use of Greek fire in the twenty-first century. Every person on Earth thought that Greek fire was a myth. They were wrong. Greek fire is used commonplace nowadays. It was the Neo-Ottoman flag again. The room caught on fire, yet Thanasis Rigas escaped slyly.

The second time was caught on security records, and Thanasis Rigas was promptly arrested, but the image of the burning of the Neo-Ottoman flag was an image that would live in infamy for centuries to come. He was arrested and put in jail with a life sentence. There has yet to be an act of terrorism that horrible in the Neo-Ottoman Empire so far. The image was captured, and is put up anonymously as part of protests against the Neo-Ottoman Empire constantly. You can see Thanasis Rigas in the picture, standing next to the burning flame that encompassed the Neo-Ottoman Empire's flag. He stood next to it, as if he was admiring his work. In the picture, he is still holding the leftover match with Greek fire in it. Thanasis Rigas was wearing a hoodie draped over his head, and on that jacket, there was a symbol. A symbol that no jacket has borne since then, hopefully. It

vas a Golden Dawn logo. That logo now rules over what used to be the
glorious Neo-Ottoman Empire. The Golden Dawn was once a terrorist
organization, and is now the most powerful country in the world. This
development was not made fairly, and should never have happened in the
first place.

I have developed a sort of "morning routine" throughout the time
that I have been stuck at this airport. I will wake up in the Netherlands-
themed room with all of my stuff strewn awry across the floor. I get up from
the uncomfortable bench and put on my disguise. It takes a while to perfect
my hair and coat to make me look like Nozdryova Lisenka Kirillovna. I will
then take a good chunk of my time packing my stuff into my large
backpack. I will take the knapsack and walk on over to the convenience
store, and get there thirty minutes before it opens. I will sit down and have a
breakfast tube. Then, my day will start.

I can not live like this for much longer. This daily routine is tiring
and tedious. I can not believe I actually miss Istanbul. Anyway, today, I will
check the flight prices to Tuvalu from Sarajevo.

I stomped into the room, and all eyes turned towards me, the female Soviet officer looking person. I stared past the glaring eyeballs, and walked towards the desk. The desk was nice, it was made out of marble, premium marble. The line was long. People were staring at me, yet no one moved. It felt good to have a sense of power back in my life. When I was an heir to the Neo-Ottoman Empire's throne, people respected me. People enjoyed my presence. But most of all, people feared me. It was good to finally have that back.

The wait in the line was long, so I <u>disgracefully</u> chewed and munched on a snack tube. Oh, goodness! You could hear the noise all the way down in Damascus! I have never been more peasant-like in my entire life than in that terribly odd moment. Soon enough, it was my turn.

I walked up to the desk and put my elbows a top it like a Serbian boy with no manners! I had just waltzed into the room and acted like a complete peasant, like a vagrant even. If my father could see me right then (I hope he could not), he would ask why I had not died. Goodness! It is fun to act like a bumpkin, at least for a bit. I then straightened myself and started conversing.

"Good morning," I said as if I had nowhere else to be and could afford to waste time on pleasantries, which, at the time, was true. I was also nailing my heavy Russian accent.

"It is the afternoon, ma'am. How may I help you today?" the rude male worker asked.

Goodness, it was the afternoon already? "I would like flight pricing please."

"From Sarajevo to where?" the man looked ready to search through his ungodly machine.

"I would like flight pricing from Sarajevo, the Bosnian Kingdom to Funafuti, Tuvalu please, sir." I asked, enunciating each and every syllable and sound that were in the words, "In Bosnian Convertible Marks."

"Funafuti, Tuvalu? I have never heard of that before? I'll check," the man said, surprised at the place I wanted to go.

A few minutes later he looked up, "The flight prices are seven-thousand-one-hundred and eighty-nine Bosnian Convertible Marks to go to Tuvalu in First Class next time there is a plane arriving. That is round-trip."

I was slightly discouraged, "What about one-way?"

He looked back down at his machine, "Three-thousand-seven-hundred-sixty-seven Bosnian Convertible Marks for a one-way flight to Funafuti, Tuvalu from Sarajevo, the Bosnian Kingdom in First Class."

"May I purchase tickets now?" I asked, knowing I had more than enough money to buy the tickets.

"Yes, you may. The card reader is ready."

I pulled out my enormous bag of cash, which grew since I had gotten more money from the store that I worked at twenty-four-seven. "Just give me a second to count it all out."

The crowd behind me in line groaned, most left. The man behind the counter groaned as well, "Go ahead."

179

As I counted out my large amount of cash, the man distracted himself. He played with his name plate. Apparently, his name was Semir Savić. Semir then went on to hum a tune as he tapped his fingers correspondingly in tune. I started to hum as well, and that is when the Semir stopped. Semir looked about thirty or forty years old, yet he acted like he was only two years of age. He played around with anything on his desk, as a person who was only two years of age would do. He threw and caught things that should not be thrown or caught, such as a glass cup. Whoever had to deal with that *child* at the end of the day was quite unlucky.

I finally finished counting the money, "There you are Semir Savić, there is eleven-thousand-seven-hundred and thirty Turkish Liras," I pulled out an extra hundred Turkish Lira bill and handed it to him, and he looked stunned. "Here is an extra hundred Turkish Liras for you for your time. Thank you. Have a wondrously good day!" I said like a common boor or lout who had too many manners and did not know how to even use them.

"Thank you very much for the tip. I have you booked for a flight from Sarajevo, the Bosnian Kingdom to Funafuti, Tuvalu in First Class at 10:30 AM. I hope you enjoy your flight to Tooraloo." He continued to marvel at the bill, amazed that someone actually gave him a tip.

I have my ticket from Sarajevo, the Bosnian Kingdom to Funafuti, Tuvalu. I have finally done it. I have finally gotten the actual ticket to escape society and to escape my life. But, what was the point? If I had revealed myself outside of the New Greek Empire, I could have regained control of the entire empire. I could have had the respect and power I always yearned for. Yet, I had chosen to escape and go on the run, for what? Society was not that bad. No! I must remember the horrid landscapes of Istanbul and all other cities in the Neo-Ottoman Empire. People threatened to kill me when I said the wrong thing in a speech. When I was a young lass, I was put on the front page of the news for weeks straight because I yawned during one of Izzet Osman's speech. I yawned because I was tired and had not eaten that day, not because I was disregarding my father. Alas, the public didn't care. The public only saw what the media fed them, and the media fed them a lot. The media constantly bottle fed the babies that were the public until they were satisfied, and then, they gave them more and more that they could not take in, yet the media continues feeding the babies until they are satisfied, and then, they continue to feed them even more. What you end up with is a bunch of babies who expect to be bottle fed information that they care deeply about, so when they're fed unimportant information, they make it important.

Society <u>sucks</u>. Society does not allow you to speak your mind. I criticize *free speech*, yet in the end, *free speech*, not constant government surveillance and constant arrests, is what keeps people in line. When people are allowed to speak their mind, they are allowed to help change the world.

181

When people can state their opinions, no matter how trivial and dumb they may be, it gets the point across to the government. Stop doing this. Start doing that. With this power, citizens are able to help the government. If the Swiss in Switzerland continued to say the Alps should be ceded back to Switzerland, then the French would catch on. Who knows, maybe the French would agree. Then, the Alps would be ceded back to Switzerland. Then, a problem would be actually solved. Then, something would be made better. If no one had spoken up, then no one would have known about the problem in the first place. Without *free speech*, the public and its citizens can not tell the media to stop. In the Neo-Ottoman Empire, you could not say that you were not interested in one news story over one other. If the public was able to say that they did not want the useless news, the public would not get the useless news. With the input from society, through *free speech*, things can get done. Governments can change how their citizens want and citizens can have a government they want. *Free speech* allows for actual change to happen.

But, the public misuses *free speech*, the public uses it like a toy. In America, people are constantly saying they want this and that and that. The American government can not keep up with so many requests. The American government ignores *free speech*, even when it is important. The American public's opinion is shoved down the unsuspecting government's throat constantly. Too much *free speech* is a bad thing. Once, in a disgraceful and controversial move, the Neo-Ottoman Empire tried to implement basic *free speech*. It was just for one month, what could happen?

In the first week, the public loved *free speech*. They were using *free speech* left and right. The first thing that was criticized? The first thing that was criticized was the choice to have the house of Osman as an absolute monarchy. That meant that the government took a hard blow immediately. By the second week in, people realized that it was unreasonable to change all of the government. The public started protesting little things. At this time, plastic cups, straws, and other utensils and accessories were still being mass-produced and mass-used.

In the second week of this experiment, the public asked the government to pull back most major plastic products that were still in use. This seemed like a good thing. An insignificant change that would please the people and help the environment at the same time. But, people took it too far. Major plastic-producing companies did not like these protests and bribed the government. The public saw this and went into an outrage. Major protests started. The protests were against the major plastic-producing companies in the Neo-Ottoman Empire. The government developed a plan to reduce most plastic usage. The public did not think that that was enough.

It was the third week, and the public was fired up. This was about the same time that a minor war genocide occurred on the border between the countries of Syria and Saudi Arabia. The genocide was not the first and was certainly not the last of the genocides in the war between the Neo-Ottoman Empire and the Saudi Arabian Kingdom. The public got upset about this as well. The public stayed quiet in the third week for the most part, as they were waiting for the fourth week to carry out their plan that they had made.

183

The fourth week came, and it was the final week. The Neo-Ottoman Empire's government was more than ready to abandon the whole *free speech* prospect. Then, four days before the last day of the month, a march started. A march of protesters, who walked all the way from the capital of the short-lived country of Turkey, Ankara to the capital of the Neo-Ottoman Empire, Istanbul. Istanbul is where all of the major Neo-Ottoman government offices and buildings were. The walk took eighty-eight hours to complete, and four different people died trying to take the walk. Once the protesters finally got to Istanbul, they protested like no humans or robots or any things had protested before.

They protested against plastic usage and they protested against the minor genocide. These things were not majorly important things usually. The public misused *free speech* to such a point that the government had to evacuate the capital. Soon, the trial period for *free speech* was over. Every single protester who participated was arrested that day.

Society still sucks. They ask for privileges such as *free speech*, and they misuse them. The public does not know how to properly act and never will. Society is horrible. I am decided, I am escaping the horrible public known as society and going to Tuvalu, where society is so undeveloped and pure, that the public knows how to act and the government is not corrupt.

I can not wait for my First Class flight to my safehaven.

Chapter Fifteen

Jackson is a pretty good city as far as I can tell so far. Whilst the streets may not be filled with the same level of hustle, bustle, and overall busyness, the streets of Jackson are still very much filled. Jackson is a city where everyone has a place to be and nobody wants to interact. Jackson is a city where everyone is cold, yet the climate is very hot.

Everyone else in my family loves this absolutely crazy place. I do not. Jackson loves Jackson, more than anyone else. He was named after where he was born, the city of Jackson, Mississippi. He loves everything about the city. Kevin and Keith are disappointed. Dallas has been sleeping since we got off of the plane and went into the airport.

I have a gotten a lay of the land over the airport. I am currently in the airport, looking through the windows to see the life on the streets. There is a street vendor directly across from here, selling *real* food. He is selling an Icelandic/New Yorkian delicacy commonly found on every street, known unofficially as hot dogs. They look disgusting.

To the right of the boarding area is the landing area, where I came from. Past the boarding area is a long hallway which can only lead to something good. I walked up to my mother and asked.

"Mother, may I explore down and past that hallway over there?" I asked politely, as my mother took her eyes off of her book.

"Do whatever you would like, just make sure to take some people with you. Everyone else is here with me. It is too tiring. Take Kevin, Keith, Jackson, Johnson, and maybe even Dallas."

"That is a lot of people to take with me. Can I just leave Johnson and Jackson with you?"

"I am being nice, Austin. I am not telling you to take any of your sisters, who I know you absolutely hate. Just take them down the hall, I can not deal with all of you with no help. Just try and enjoy yourself and help the others enjoy themselves. That was the whole reason for the trip," my mother responded blatantly, immediately going back to her book.

I took everyone with me. By everyone, I mean the people my mother asked me to bring with me: Kevin, Keith, Jackson, Johnson and Dallas. I was most upset about Dallas and Jackson. Dallas was the largest idiot on the surface of this Earth, and Jackson has never been more excited to visit a city, especially the city that he was named after. We have visited the city of Jackson, Mississippi before, but this time, Jackson was more excited than ever before. Jackson was giddy with joy and hope, even more than usual. Jackson's personality was in stark contrast to Johnson's, especially on this specific visit to Jackson, Mississippi.

Jackson and Johnson are twins, both born in Jackson, Mississippi when my parents went on a vacation there alone. Somehow, every vacation we have had as a family, and my parents have had just alone has been in the quaint and annoyingly rude city of Jackson, Mississippi. I thought that, just his once, since we were actually voting on which city, we would go to anywhere but the quaint and annoyingly rude city of Jackson, Mississippi. I was wrong.

Anyway, Jackson and Johnson's personalities are very different. As you have probably noticed by now. Jackson is peppy and giddy and always constantly excited over nothing. He is like an excitable Chihuahua who thinks that every day is the best day. Jackson's vocabulary is limited, with him relying on words such as dingus, ain't (an abbreviation for the phrases do not, does not, did not, am not, is not, are not, has not, and have not). Meanwhile, Johnson is a serious and conceited individual. He is constantly correcting people, which gave him the nickname of "actually." His vocabulary was not limited, unlike Jackson's.

That was not a fun time during walking down the corridor. The corridor was lined with a bunch of random quotes and odds and ends. There was an outline map of Africa covered with an elephant, which looked like something a two year old would dream of. There was a lot of surreal and abstract art. There was one picture that was just a bunch of meaningless dots on a white background accompanied by the artist's signature. Every single picture was abstract and made absolutely no sense. The last picture in the surprisingly interminably long corridor. It was a humongous picture of text colored in rainbow coloring. It read:

187

Ideology Poem

Capitalism is distribution based on greed

Socialism is distribution based on need

Communism is distribution based on deeds

Conservatism is distribution based on who is already freed

Theocracy is rule based on church

Nazism is rule based on your birth

Fascism is rule based on one's sense of your worth

Egalitarianism is rule based on no one's worth

Autocracy is rule based on one's own view of their self-worth

Absolutism has a government ruler that is only one

Anarchism has a government ruler that is none

Monarchism has a government ruler that is a proper one

Dictatorship has a government ruler that is not a proper one

Democracy has a government ruler that is everyone

Imperialism wants everything to be under them

Nationalism wants everything to be free from them

Totalitarianism is constant surveillance of the population

Oligarchy is a rule by only a small population

Aristocracy is a division of power in the economy to only a small population

Authoritarianism is a rule where freedoms are given to no population

I enjoyed that "poem" that described basic ideologies. Although it may not have been the most descriptive descriptions of basic ideologies. I decided to write a list of countries that identified as different things, knowing Jackson, Johnson, Kevin, Keith, and Dallas ran around the entire expansive Jackson airport.

America is capitalist, imperialist, democratic, and aristocratic. I guess that is a good thing? I mean, imperialism may not be such a good thing. Imperialism has never been an admirable quality in countries in the past. The Japanese Empire started in 1868, and was hated until it ended 1947. They killed tens of thousands of people in Korea and Japan during World War Two. They are now always regarded as a horrible empire with terrifying intentions.

Many countries are fascist nowadays. During its limited existence, the Neo-Ottoman Empire was a fascist dictatorship (according to American newspapers I read), and it was hated for i's rule. It was ruled by the descendants of the House of Osman. Recently, the government of the Neo-Ottoman Empire collapsed, and was taken over by Greek rebels and reformed into the New Greek Empire. Attached below in my journal is an article summarizing the conquest of the Neo-Ottoman Empire and the takeover by the New Greek Empire. I found this specific article on the plane in my seat pocket in the middle of a lifestyle magazine, hence why it is only a very quick summary of what actually happened.

The Neo-Ottoman Empire is Gone. Long Live the House of Osman!

Greek rebels killed the sultan of the Neo-Ottoman Empire, Izzet Osman, in late December. The heir to the throne, Maurie Osman, is currently suspected to be on the run. The rebellion that took over the Neo-Ottoman Empire was Golden Dawn. Golden Dawn has been trying for decades to reunite the Byzantine Empire, and they finally succeeded.

The Golden Dawn rebellion has changed greatly over the years. It started as an ultranationalist, far right political organization in Greece that was up for election in the Greek government. Where the far right political party once stood, a terrorist organization formed. And where that terrorist organization once stood, a rebellion soon formed. And where that rebellion once stood, the New Greek Empire sits. The Golden Dawn has always been an ideocratic authoritative state, with its government acting the exact opposite of America's. The New Greek Empire has also been accused of totalitarianist actions.

The invasion was one of many that were consistently happening in Istanbul. The Golden Dawn organization had launched a plan to have scheduled weekly invasions. Although it was just a regular invasion, this time was different. This time, the Golden Dawn organization had laid out a plan. The Neo-Ottoman Empire and its sultan did not expect the Golden

Dawn organization to actually be prepared, so, as usual, they sent no army to counterattack. The Golden Dawn started invading near the Bosphorus, and destroyed the heir to the throne's mansion, and they suspected they killed her. Then, they went past the remains of Maurie Osman's mansion and towards Izzet Osman's mansion. This did not take a while, as they expected, and Izzet Osman was gone before anyone knew it, right next to his daughter and their mansions.

The New Greek Empire was then formed, and a ruler was established six days later. The ruler was known as Dimos Vassallos, who was the founder of the rebellion that actually took over the Neo-Ottoman Empire. Although it was still part of the Golden Dawn organization, it was a separate wing that he had created. He won by a surprising landslide after a vote in mainland Greece. He was shot on the night of his first speech. Next in line was Qamar Gabris, who was on that stage and shot less than three seconds after Dimos Vassallos was shot.

After two rulers had been shot, the shooters were arrested. Next in line was Antonis Melis. While Dimos Vassallos was a neutral ideocratic, Qamar Gabris and Antonis Melis both picked their sides, mainly because they created them. Qamarianism and Antoniaism are types of ideocratic ideologies created by Qamar Gabris and Antonis Melis respectively.

Although it may seem like that is the end of the story, it is not. The person who shot Dimos Vassallos was Maurie Osman. When checked into prison, she admitted herself as Gennadiya Petrov, a Georgian refugee who hated Greek politics. She was later put in solitary confinement when she was found with a gun. The Istanbul prison (where she was kept) admitted to have planted two people who had committed crimes with a gun to give to Maurie Osman in a deal that let the criminals walk away free.

In solitary confinement, Maurie Osman did not last long. She was given a knife to cut a pineapple, and she used that knife to later escape from her cell. She is currently on the loose and has not been spotted yet. If you see anyone resembling Maurie Osman or Gennadiya Petrov, please contact your local police or the Greek police.

It is interesting following international news, especially the new of the New Greek Empire, since all of the controversy rose about. I wonder what it would be like to meet Maurie Osman. I wonder what she was thinking when she decided to create her fake identity of Gennadiya Petrov. I wonder what she was thinking when she broke out of prison using a pineapple knife. She must be quite clever.

Anyways, I got back up from the bench I had been on, looking at the poem, and walked over to Dallas. Dallas was looking through a magazine that was not so appropriate for him. I left him alone. Jackson and Johnson were looking at touristy stuff, like they did on every vacation, yet they never actually bought anything. Johnson would always say he wanted to save his money, and that would upset Jackson, so then Jackson would not buy anything to show how "responsible" he could be. Jackson always got upset afterwards. Kevin and Keith were rambunctiously playing tag, running past and around strangers.

I decided not to intervene in any of those situations, and went on ver to the help desk. I found the help desk easily, as there was a giant red ign that said "help desk" in big white letters, probably the **BOLD)SWALD** font. It caught my eye, and I headed over there.

I arrived at the desk, "Hello."

A man turned around, with a familiar smile, and a familiar crispy aircut, "How can I help you, Austin?"

I was dumbfounded, standing at the foot of my father's desk. Here e was, at an airport in Jackson, Mississippi as a help desk employee. How ad I not seen this before? My father needed his constant supply of arcotics, and my mother hated that. My mother made him move out under he false pretense that he was dead. He then bought and opened up a onvenience store in Minneapolis, right next to the old one that my family vent to. He changed his hair, giving him that crispy hairspray hair that I had lescribed. Who was my manager at the convenience store? No one other han my own father. My father bought the store, and hired me without taking second glance at me or my resume. Just because he changed his vest and is hair does not mean I should not have recognized him.

I stood there, across from him, as we both waited for the other to omment. My father left my family. Why would I be nice to him after that? I stared him down, as sweat dripped off of his forehead, from the hot climate. I could stand here like this forever. My father looked at me, knowing that I had figured out who he was. He looked at me with a look of impatience. As if, as if, he had no time for me. As if he did not care that he did not tell us he was leaving when he did. He had grown tall and thin, and looked paler than before. He had thinned, from a lack of food. He looked as though he could collapse any second. He looked like someone you would expect to be addicted to drugs. He lowered his glasses, shining the sunlight from the sunroof directly above him down onto me and my clothes.

He still waited. I still waited. He wore neon clothes, looking the exact opposite of when he was my father, when he always wore all-black. His vest was gargantuan next to the shell of a man that he was. He bought a store just to avoid his family, and now, he was in Jackson, Mississippi. His figure and stature were laughable, which was in stark contrast to how he used to be. His figure changing represented himself changing. He had gone from laudable to laughable. He had used my name, so maybe he did want to see me.

I broke the silence, and it was a relief to my ears, "Why on Earth are you here?" A good start to a horrible conversation that was soon to erupt in the airport's already quiet and fragile atmosphere.

He pulled his glasses back up. He straightened his vest. He looked at me directly, "You know. You're a smart kid. You have figured it out. I hope you enjoy the convenience store."

I straightened myself, mimicking his posture, or thereof lack of. I mirrored him, raising my head up, and lowering my standards down, "Well. You are a help desk employee an-"

He interrupted me mid-sentence, smiling at what I had said, "That I am. How can i help you today?"

I looked towards him, he looked towards me. I decided that I could let this go for this second, "What are the flight prices to Funafuti, Tuvalu from Jackson, Mississippi, lowest class?"

He looked confused, "Why are you going to Funafuti, Tooraloo?"

"I believe that is none of your business as a random help desk employee in Jackson, Mississippi," I said, lowering myself to his despicable level. I stared him down until he spoke again.

He looked up at me and put his hands on his desk, "I believe that would be important if I am going to give you free tickets?"

"Excuse me?" I asked.

"You're my son. I support you. Why are you going to Fun-a-fu-tthi, Tooraloo, Austin?"

"To escape and t-" I started.

"Say no more," he interrupted once again, "Here are your tickets from Jackson, Mississippi to Fratooti, Toovenloaf, in First Class. Enjoy." He handed me two tickets, one for the way there, and one for the way back.

I took the tickets, and winked. My father winked back. I looked back before leaving, "Why Jackson, Mississippi?"

"Memories."

Right before I left, he shouted one last thing, "Have fun in Funafuti, Tooraloo!"

His old and frail figure did not change him at all. Those words were the last thing I would ever hear out of my father's mouth. A mispronunciation of my new home country was the last word that my father ever said (shouted) to (at) me.

Chapter Sixteen

First Class is different than I expected. I assumed First Class in the Bosnian Kingdom would be the same as in America. I had only learned about First Class in America. It is a different cabin near the front of the plane (odd, considering the front is more dangerous; would people not want to pay more for a safer flight?), with high class services and goods. Amazing, home-cooked food is provided to you, but alas, it will never taste as good as it would have on the ground. Taste buds and smell are the first things that go once you reach nine point one-four-four kilometers in the air. In America, instead of eating a meal or snack tube, they actually provide you with real food and stuff in First Class only. You have a bunch of ungodly machines to use at your leisure, and they are equipped with movies. The seats are wider and much more comfortable, and they even recline. There was a point in time where First Class was too fancy. Alas, that time is gone. First Class has declined in the United States of America.

First Class may have declined in the United States of America, but it increased in quality in the Bosnian Kingdom. It turns out that you get your own plane, just for you and all of the other people willing to schmooze the extra money out of their pockets just to show that they are fancier. The seats on First Class planes in the Bosnian Kingdom are unbelievable. First off, they are spaced about three meters apart, which is insanely expensive! Second off, they are literal couches that expand into beds! Finally, there are no ungodly machines shoved into your face! It is wondrous! There are many, many, many magazines and newspapers to read. Throughout most of the flight, I have just been reading all of the magazines and newspapers. However, there is one thing I have yet to mention that makes this the best flight I have and will ever be on. I am the only one on this plane!

It turns out that no one really wants to go to the wondrous place known as Funafuti, Tuvalu, which I will soon call home. I wonder which areas have the most plane traffic nowadays. Definitely not the Taiwanese Dynasty, no one goes there. Maybe America does. America has thirteen different major cities to brag about, and they are all good tourist destinations. Plus, flights are sometimes cheaper throughout America. France would be my second guess. Despite decades of war, the Neo-French Empire is still a touristy place, even without the Eiffel Tower. Paris is no longer the most visited city, but Nantes is. Nantes is very far away from any borders that may actually cause trouble to tourists.

I am worried. Niue's government is an absolute cult, yet I do not know if Tuvalu's government is a cult. Tuvalu could just be an island in the middle of nowhere with no population. Nauru is abandoned, Tuvalu could just as well be abandoned. I sure do hope that Tuvalu is a place I could actually live for the rest of my life. I am going to take a walk and see how I feel afterwards. With all of the plane being empty, it will be easy to walk around without ignoring anyone.

"Hello, I was wondering how long it will be until we land in Funafuti," I asked, as I walked up to one of the only flight attendants.

"Hello there, ma'am. It seems that we will first have to land in the city of Angelo, in the United States of America to switch off from our high-speed First Class flight service to the regular service provided in the United States of America. In the United States of America, high-speed planes are not available. We only have enough fuel to go to Angelo, then, we will end up in Funafuti after a normal-speed flight, where, of course, you will be transferred in to First Class. In the meantime, we hope you enjoy your flight. If you would like," the flight attendant took a breath, as a human being on this idiotic Earth would, "you could meet our wonderful pilot once he has a chance to put the plane on autopilot," the flight attendant said.

"How long until this plane lands in the city of Angelo, California in the United States of America?" I asked, hoping that it would not be too long until I could get to Tuvalu.

"Only about less than nine hours until we land in Angelo. In the meantime, our pilot will be putting the plane on autopilot."

"Why do you keep talking about the pilot?"

"I am sorry, I have to go and cook."

"I did not order anything -"

She walked away quickly. I began to worry. Was there a pilot? I did not know at this point. I walked back to my seat, slowly. I did not even get halfway there before I heard the plane falling.

199

It was a slow noise at first. My ears popped immediately. I fell down, the cabin pressure changed, and I screamed. I screamed because my father died, I screamed because my empire had collapsed, I screamed because Ari was a traitor, I screamed because Shegan gave me a pineapple knife for some reason, I screamed because I hate Sarajevo and the Bosnian Kingdom itself, I screamed because the flight was so expensive, I screamed because the plane was falling and I could not do anything to stop it, and I screamed because I never even met my mother, and I no longer have any parents.

I screamed because society sucks, I screamed because society told me to die every day, I screamed because society hates the government, I screamed because everything sucks.

I ran towards the pilot's seat. Autopilot was not on. The flight attendant tried to stop me. I pushed past her, and ran towards the pilot seat. The door was locked. Now was the time when learning lock picking would have been useful, and luckily, I had. I was wondering when it would actually pay off. I reached into my Soviet coat pockets. Nothing was in them except for a napkin. I was absolutely and positively screwed at that point in time.

I rushed back to my seat. I had opened a snack tube earlier and closed the bag to save what was left. What did I close it with? Nothing other han a paperclip. I went down the other aisle, so the flight attendant would not try and stop me. Paperclip in hand, I fell to my knees at the pilot's door. The plane continued to drop. My ears popped again. My hair was flying everywhere. I had to hold on to the seat next to me just to stay on the ground.

The flight attendant slid down the other aisle, defeated by gravity. The plane dropped another hundred meters or so. My stuff went flying across the plane. I held my hand steady with my other hand and tried to desperately pick the lock. I felt around the insides of the lock, and got the paperclip in. I stood up. The plane dropped another hundred meters or so. I fell down and into the door, which swung open forwards into the cockpit, as I involuntarily slid into them. I was finally inside of the cockpit. There was no one there.

Who had flown the plane at first? Had the flight attendant started flying and then came and assisted me. I stood upright again, and leaned against the wall nearest to me. The plane fell yet another hundred meters. I slumped down again, defeated by the force of gravity. The plane stabilized a bit, and I got up. The door to the wires was wide open, exposing a cut wire. The flight attendant had cut the autopilot wire. I crawled towards the small opening. There was barely enough room for me. I held the wires together using my hand.

Electricity sparked and flew, it had worked, and I was holding the remnants of the wire close enough for them to conduct. The plane dropped yet again another hundred meters or so. I flew down to the edge of the cockpit, like a lifeless body. My head throbbed with searing pain. I stood up yet again and crawled, holding close to the ground. The plane dropped again yet another hundred meters or so. I grabbed on to the chair and pulled myself towards the wire opening.

My fingers were not going to work properly to conduct the electricity in the wire properly and for as long as I would need it to in order to press the autopilot button. What did I have or see that was conductive? I reached back into my pocket, where I had put my paperclip from before.

I took it out and reached towards the opening. The plane dropped again. My ears popped, and I hit my head on the wall of the cockpit. I was dazed, and it took me a second to regain my plan for what I was doing. I reached for the paper clip again and clinged to the floor as I crawled. The plane stabilized somewhat. I ran-crawled towards the wire opening with my paperclip. I tucked the paperclip in on one end, and then did the same to the other end. I held the paperclip into the wires for a few seconds, and then let go. The electricity sparked and sparks flew. The button was working again. How simple it was, that all I had to do to actually save my life at this point was to hit a small red button.

Without hesitation, I hit the button. The plane stabilized. Autopilot nowadays is highly comprehensive and impressive. Autopilot nowadays works better than pilots do, and it is usually cheaper. Pilots are just there for extra safety and security, and to make official announcements to the passengers. I relaxed and started breathing normally. In and out. I took many deep breaths before I returned to my seat. The flight attendant had been

nocked out cold, as she had it her head really hard when gravity defeated
ier and pulled her down against the heavy metal door in the right aisle.

It was a while before I finally returned to my seat. Once I got there, I
tarted writing this journal entry.

I picked up my stuff and returned it to my seat. I set everything down
iefore I went back to the pilot's cabin. Once I got there, I looked towards
he main monitor to see how much time I had left before I landed. The main
nonitor was broken, and I did not expect that for some reason. I decided to
ust sit down and wait until the plane finally landed in Angelo, California.

I just had a near-death experience. Normally, people will say that
hey appreciate their life and how they are living right after they have a
iear-death experience, but I was not appreciating my life any more than I
ilready had. To be fair, I have had many near-death experiences and death
hreats, so this is not that much of a change. Last time, when I was in prison,
f that actually counts as a near-death experience, I was so used to it that I
iarely even thought about it. The time before that, when my mansion was
ibliterated by Golden Dawn, I was the closest I had ever been to dying. The
ihots were not that far off from me or my body. I could have easily died in
that moment, and yet, I feel as if that is normal for me.

I appreciate my life and I love that I am able to live. I do hope that
ione of my near-death experiences actually end in death. Death is not a

subject I would like to think about, as it seems so far off, yet it will come one day whether I like it or not, and I will not expect it.

Just as I was thinking about the sad truth of the inevitability of death the plane landed. My ears popped and I was relieved. A few minutes later, the airplane door opened, and I was able to take my stuff and finally get off of that plane that nearly killed me.

I was greeted by a man in his early twenties, who seemed surprised to see an empty plane. His nametag said that his name was Christopher. Christopher is such an American name.

"Hello ma'am, did you enjoy your flight today?" Christopher asked confidently, as if he heard nothing about the plane crashing.

I stared into his eyes, hoping to intimidate him, "Sure," I lied. I knew that if word got out, that my name (Nozdryova Lisenka Kirillovna), and somehow, people would figure out that Nozdryova Lisenka Kirillovna is Gennadiya Petrov is Maurie Osman. I do not need another press story.

I walked past him and into the airport. Where I expected a horrid, average, *American* airport, I was greeted with an airport the size of the Istanbul prison. In that sense, it was humongous. The ceilings extended tens of tens of meters above anyone's head, and it seemed to be just a way to how off how large and expansive the Angelo airport truly was. Behind me nd slightly to my left there was the landing flights area, marked by a bright ed sign in a very clear and distinct font. To my far right, there was the oarding flights area. To my very far left, there was a very small help desk. 'ast the boarding flight and landing flight areas, there were stores upon tores upon stores. This airport was truly amazing.

I walked towards the help desk, where I saw a large sign that ndicated when flights were landing and when flights were taking off. My light to Funafuti was in seventeen minutes. Oh boy, did I absolutely run hrough security just to get to that flight early.

Once I got there, there was one other person waiting in line.

Chapter Seventeen

How did I get on that flight? It was a step-by-step process. First, I had to steal money from my mother's purse (you will find out why later), that step required me to go into her purse in the dark of night and grab one-hundred dollars USD. Although it was a lot, I was overestimating. The next step was me actually slipping away from my family, which was the easiest step. Right at the crack of dawn, I ran out of our hotel room, grabbed a meal tube from the lobby, and walked out of the hotel's doors and into the depths of Jackson, Mississippi. The next step was getting to the airport. I had to hitchhike. I would not recommend hitchhiking, as it is demeaning. However, no matter what, it actually gets you places. I spent about forty full minutes just trying to hitchhike and failing. I had to gradually move away from the hotel my family was staying at so that they did not spot me. Finally, I got a ride from some semi-rich guy that spoke with a horribly fake sounding American accent. I paid him generously for the ride, yet he was still very upset with the generous amount I gave him. I ran out of the guy's car with all of my stuff before he could stop me.

By then, I was at the airport. I went to the help desk and saw that my flight was boarding in a while, so I had some time to do things. First, I bought only a few essentials. I bought a bunch of snack tubes and meal tubes and snack juices, a toothbrush and toothpaste, and a book for the long plane ride. The book I got was written in German and was about tourists in southern Indonesia. I do not know why I chose that oddly specific book, but was still entertaining once I got on the flight from Jackson, Mississippi to Angelo, California.

Eventually, my flight was boarding and I ran through security. Security nowadays is a joke in airports, so it does not take much time to get through. You just have to go through a scanner and then leave. That means that you can literally run through security, as you would just have to run through the scanner itself. Once I was at the boarding flights section, I noticed that I was the only one on the flight from Jackson, Mississippi to Angelo, California.

It took a while before they let me board, but I did end up on the plane, and in First Class. Of course, I felt very *classy* in First Class. With the cushioned seats, hundreds of never-touched magazines and newspapers that are incredibly outdated at this point, and the wondrous home-cooked meals and snacks. There was also special service that made you feel like all of the special service was for you and only you. Being in First Class makes you feel special.

I unpacked my stuff and sprawled myself and all of my assorted things and stuff awry across the entirety of the First Class cabin. I was doing nothing wrong, as I was the only one in First Class. For goodness sake, I was the only one on that entire flight to Angelo, California from Jackson, Mississippi.

My backpack lay on the seat in the aisle across from me, and everything else was everywhere as well. The flight attendants were clearly annoyed by this. Since there happened to be many miniature television-like things that also had games on the comfy dark red recliner chairs that were in First Class, I decided to watch a movie, and play a game. I set up the movie and the chair in the seat across from me, where my backpack was. I set the game up on the television screen in front of me. I was watching an English soap opera, so I barely understood it. Not because it was in English (a language I can now proudly say I am absolutely and positively fluent in), but because it was a soap opera with no actual discernible plot, discernable story, discernable setting, or discernable character development arcs.

Whilst the movie was horrible, the game was fun. I had to move a cubed snake around to get to small dots, and I could not touch the snake's body against itself. Every time my digital snake absorbed a miniature dot on the miniature television-like thing, it grew bigger by only one cube. I actually turned out to be insanely good at the game, as it was quite easy and simplistic. I wonder when that game was originally made, and what it was originally called.

The comfy recliner chair was dark red and very comfy. There is not really anything else to talk about that happened during the flight. The book written in German about tourism in southern Indonesia was kind of interesting to me. Many people will travel to Bali, Ubud, Kuta, and Jakarta for pointless touristy trips. The book reflected that, and told those tourists what exactly to do in those cities. I suppose that I should not be insulting those who travel to unnecessary places with money that they do not actually have. My family has always traveled to cities such as Jackson, Mississippi or pointless and meaningless vacations. We do not gain anything from these vacations, hence why they are meaningless and pointless.

Many people will travel to Angelo, California, Cleveland, Ohio, and Anchorage, Alaska. Angelo has always been a popular tourist destination, even when it was known as the city of Los Angeles. Cleveland, Ohio is a popular tourist destination, because it is a city with lots of history and things to do. The humble city of Cleveland, Ohio is one of the most important major cities in the United States of America. When someone thinks of the United States of America, they will think of Cleveland, Ohio. When it comes to what the United States of America stereotypically looks like, the city of Cleveland, Ohio is the first city to come to mind. Finally, the very old and odd city of Anchorage, Alaska is a city that tourists flock to. It is a popular destination because Anchorage, Alaska and the entire state of Alaska is so foreign nowadays to Americans, even though it is in the United States of America. Traveling to Anchorage, Alaska is like traveling to a foreign place IN the United States of America for tourists that want to travel worldwide without the proper budget.

My family always chose Jackson because it was originally a common destination for its population. It was one of the first real major cities. My family caught on to that trend and never let that go. Then, once the twins of Jackson and Johnson were born in the city of Jackson, Mississippi, a tradition was born. Jackson and Johnson constantly wanted to go to Jackson, Mississippi over any other place because it was their namesake. The tradition was born and has been followed every time we have "extra" money to take a vacation.

Despite all of the entertainment that was offered on the flight, I was still very bored throughout all of those hours that I was in that First Class flight. The movie was the worst I had ever seen, but I suppose I should not expect better considering that it is a movie being shown on an airplane. Even with all of my excess room in First Class, and the entire plane, I still felt cramped inside of the (surprisingly comfortable) airplane. Right now, the pilot has just announced that we will land in twenty-four and a half minutes. I can not wait to get off of this plane.

I walked into the Angelo airport in Angelo, California. It looks like the worst possible stereotype of an airport in the United States of America. Construction signs are plastered everywhere, there is even a sash on top of the boarding flights sign. The sash was striped diagonally with the colors of black and yellow. It read: ***UNDER CONSTRUCTION***. It was worn like how a mayor would wear a mayoral sash. It seemed to be worn with pride, as if the Angelo airport was happy with their construction. The sign itself was apparently under construction, there was literally a hole in the upper right corner.

To add to the excessive amount of unnecessary construction all throughout the airport, in the boarding flight area, the landing flight area, the elp desk area, and the shopping area, the quality of everything was epressing. The help desk was wooden, for Pete's sake. The stores were all najor corporations, such as medicinal pharmacies and convenience stores. he floors were dirty beyond belief. This entire place disgusts me extremely o.

 To add to that, the airport is very tall. It was like forty-seven yards all. It just kept going. The airport was extravagant in that sense, but it was uch a waste of money if they were not going to build another floor or nything. It was just extra, empty space. The extra forty-seven yards of pace that went far past everyone in the airport's heads represented how nuch the United States of America spends on unnecessary things. Overall, he Angelo airport is the most stereotypical airport in America. When one hinks of an *American* airport, they will think of the Angelo airport. With its onstant construction, horrible maintenance, depressing architecture, and ad smell, it was truly the *American* airport.

 I walked up to the help desk, where there was an LED board that illuminated the flight landing times and flight boarding times. Of course, it was a bad machine. The lights flickered constantly, and half of the names were misspelled. According to the LED board, the flight from Chicago to Angelo would land in four and half hours. I had to stand there for a while, just trying to read the boarding time of the flight to Funafuti, Tuvalu. I had just about half of an hour until the flight from Angelo, California to Funafuti, Tuvalu boarded. I have lots of extra time.

    I am at a bench next to a "cafe." In other news, I just learned what a "cafe" is. A "cafe" is a place where food is served, and people, just, kind of, sit there. Some people will write or read. Others will talk with others. Most will sit just to take a break from their lives. It is a weird concept. The cafe I went to is called *Starbucks*. It makes sense, considering that this food-serving concept thing makes no money, so all of their money is up in the stars. In the cafe, two people are reading the news. One person is reading an actual book. Finally, there is a very small group of people having a light conversation. I ended up just grabbing coffee and sitting outside with coffee writing in my journal. I am writing about what I have been doing for the past twenty minutes of the thirty minutes I have before my flight from Angelo, California to Funafuti, Tuvalu boards. I am very excited to finally escape society.

    As well as going to *Starbucks*, I also went to a pharmacy. It turns out that medicine for the Uruguayan Influenza is sold in Angelo, California. I was able to withdraw just enough money for me to buy medicine for the Uruguayan Influenza for a couple of months. I would now actually be able to survive in Funafuti, Tuvalu for a couple of months. I was beginning to notice symptoms of my Uruguayan Influenza acting up again, so it is good

hat I got me medicine while I could. With all of the money I have spent so
ar, it will take a miracle for me NOT to go bankrupt. I really hope I do not
crew up my own adventure with my money, or lack thereof. My money
roblems are, at this moment, unfortunately, the least of my concerns, of
vhich I happened to have a lot. But first and foremost, is how I am going to
et on the next flight on time.

I walked towards security, and the scanners themselves were in very
ad shape. Those scanners could not detect metal if it was the only thing
hey did, which it was. Those scanners could not even detect metal if it was
vaved in front of their very visible sensors. Those scanners were depressing.
uckily, I actually was able to get through security and their scanners. Once
got through the "security" line (if you could even call it security), I was
net with the sight of an empty line for the flight from Angelo, California to
unafuti, Tuvalu.

I waited for a while, and just relaxed for a second. I had about five or
o minutes until the plane actually boarded. Soon, someone started towards
he line that only I was in. Was someone else going to Funafuti, Tuvalu?
Was Tuvalu NOT a safehaven? Was Tuvalu a tourist's destination? Why
was this person even going to the unknown country of Tuvalu?

The person in question was a tall female who seemed to be just about
my age. She had dirty blonde hair, put into a frizzy, loose hairstyle. She was

wearing a heavy Russian/Soviet coat. She walked towards me, not looking too enthused to see another person on a flight to Funafuti, Tuvalu.

"Hello," she said, "Why are you flying to Funafuti?"

"Why is that your business?" I shot back.

"Because I need to escape society, and you, just like everyone else, are mostly a painful reminder of everything wrong in society. Why are you flying to Funafuti, Tuvalu?" She asked, glaring at me, seemingly trying to intimidate me. I would not fall for it at all.

"How do you know I am not searching for a safehaven?" I asked coyly.

"What could you have to escape from?" She responded blatantly, as if she couldn't fathom others having problems.

"Why do you think you are the only one who has things to escape from?"

"Well, I had to escape from a lot."

"What did you have to escape from? What could have possibly troubled you in Siberia?"

"How do you know I am from Siberia?"

"You're wearing a heavy Soviet coat."

"I had to escape from political problems."

"Fine." I said, defeated. Maybe I could try and make friends, we were both trying to find a safehaven.

"Why did you have to escape?"

I lied and said, "Political problems as well."

"Why Tuvalu?"

"It was the only country in the atlas that I did not know. How did ou find the country of Tuvalu?"

"I found the country's name on a coin," she said, as she pulled out a usty coin from her pocket with some sort of space-themed logo, "Yes, it is 1 fact an entirely real coin."

"Interesting. What is your name?"

"Nozdryova Lisenka Kirillovna."

"That is quite a mouthful."

"Considering we will be spending lots of time with each other, you nay call me Noz for short," I chuckled, "What is your name?"

I saw something in her eyes, a sparkle almost. It was the same eye parkle that my father got when he lied, which he did a lot. She was lying, "My name is Austin, but what is your real name?"

"Nozdryova Lisenka Kirillovna, as I said before," her eyes sparkled yet again with the same sparkle.

"We're going to be spending the rest of our lives in Tuvalu together, since we both want a safehaven because we both hate society. You might as well just tell me what your real name is. If you are someone who should be n any sort of trouble in the United States of America or even internationally, I do not care and I will not tell. I am just glad to have someone with similar values to spend my safehaven days with. You can tell me your real name."

215

Noz sighed the largest sigh possible, she rubbed her eyes for a second and then looked down at the floor, "My name is Maurie Osman."

Maurie Osman? I guess I had wondered what it would be like to meet her, "So you are escaping political troubles? And you have created another identity to go by the name of Nozdryova Lisenka Kirillovna?"

She looked upset that I knew who she was, "Yes, but now that I am meeting someone who understands my need to escape from society, I have to reveal who I really am."

"Well, thank you. I can not wait to escape society with you. You seem like a good person, so I will not contact any authorities. We are both just looking for an escape, an escape from society."

"Well, on the hope of moving away from both of our histories with society, what do you think Tuvalu is going to look like?" Maurie had calmed down entirely, "I am suspecting it will be tropical, like Hawaii or northern New Zealand."

"I agree. Since they have an airport, I suspect that their architecture and city design will be more impressive than we expected. Perhaps it will follow traditional tropical boundaries, but probably with a modern twist, or a twist emphasizing Tuvaluan culture itself."

"I think that Tuvalu would not be *that* architecturally developed. I suspect that the house style will be mainly American and overall unimpressive. The flight should be boarding soon should it not be?"

"It has been a while."

Suddenly, an announcement came over the loudspeaker, "The flight in section T-SEVEN from Angelo, California, the United States of America, to Funafuti, Tuvalu will be boarding now. I repeat, the flight in section T-SEVEN from Angelo, California, the United States of America, to Funafuti, Tuvalu will be boarding now. Those who have any physical disabilities and need assistance may board first. First Class may board next. Finally, economy class will board last. Thank you for listening and we hope you enjoy your flight from Angelo, California to Funafuti, Tuvalu, and as always, thank you for flying *CaliAIR*, the only real American airline."

"I guess we should board. I am in First Class, are you?"

"Yes indeed, and I believe we are the only ones on this flight from Angelo, California to Funafuti, Tuvalu."

We boarded the flight, and I am now on the flight from Angelo, California to Funafuti, Tuvalu. I am one plane ride away from completing my adventure, and so is Maurie Osman. I am extremely happy to have met someone. Now, I will be able to spend time with people I already know in Funafuti, Tuvalu. She has fallen asleep, with her snack tube still in her hands. I am leaving her alone. Earlier, I noticed her writing in her own journal. I wonder what she writes about. I wonder why she writes. I am ecstatic that I was able to meet someone to spend my "safehaven days" with. I will not entirely be alone on this adventure and any others that may arise for me. Also, Maurie Osman will not be alone anymore. She will now have support from me whenever she needs to escape from politics. I will now have support from her. It seems like a good plan, but I do hope that I do not screw it up.

First Class on this plane is the same as the last one, but instead of dark red chairs, they have light blue chairs. Maurie seemed surprised by First Class, and I wondered if First Class in the New Greek Empire or other parts of Europe was as good as First Class is in The United States of America.

I looked towards her, the plane had not even started moving, "Enjoying First Class so far?"

She looked somewhat confused, "This is First Class?"

Chapter Eighteen

The one other person in line was also traveling to Tuvalu. He was a short, brown-haired, *nerd* who wanted to escape his dysfunctional family. I do not condemn him for his actions, nor do I entirely support them. Just because one's family is dysfunctional does not mean you have to run off to an unknown country thousands of miles away just to escape them. Perhaps, I should not be judgmental. He could have serious family issues. Alas, he is not a presence that I can guarantee will be enjoyed in Tuvalu, nor is he the kind of presence that I can guarantee will be hated in Tuvalu. I do not like this Austin very much so far, yet I suppose I should be empathetic or sympathetic to him after all he has gone through. Although he is a nerd, he seems quite nice so far and has made the trip enjoyable. He understands what I am going through, in some sense, and he is trying to make everything easier for me. Whilst I do appreciate his kindness, he must know that he must treat me like an everyday human being, so that the people of Tuvalu do not find out who I really am.

I suspect I will use the Nozdryova Lisenka Kirillovna identity in Tuvalu. While it may be hard to keep up, I will not have to keep up those shenanigans when Austin is around. I forgot to mention, I have indeed told Austin who I really am. He dragged it out of me in a vulnerable time. Alas, I should never be that trustworthy of someone ever again. I have now handed the fate of my fragile future into the worst hands I could have: a twenty-two year old know-it all from Austin, Texas who is too nice to ever actually lie about anything.

I hope that I will be able to leave him behind in some way. I should stop talking about this Austin No-Last-Name-Because-He-Does-Not-Know-For-Some-Reason as if I am obsessed with him, which I am very much NOT. Honestly, I may escape Tuvalu to some other random place like Niue or Nauru just to escape the one person who knows who I really am.

On the topic of a very different subject, First Class in the United States of America is very different than in the Bosnian Kingdom. On the flight from Sarajevo, the Bosnian Kingdom to Angelo, the United States of America, as I wrote earlier, First Class had its very own plane. With comfy pull-out beds that were spaced three entire freaking meters apart, the plane was insanely luxurious! With home-cooked food and that whole shabang to add to it, First Class in the Bosnian Kingdom makes you feel very special. In the United States of America, First Class is much less luxurious. With dark red, somehow uncomfortable, blood-color seats, meals cooked **IN** the plane, and ungodly machines strapped haphazardly onto the backs of the disgustingly-colored seats. Ugh! Machines do not belong in the same world as proper acting human beings who actually have a real brain.

The machine was a telly combined with a game-machine. It was a two-in-one to simplify. I did not dare to touch it, so I do not know how it exactly worked. Machines in the modern world, on a highly accessible plane? Who are we? Are we barbarians from the Taiwanese Dynasty? Why would anyone in their right mind put one of those ungodly machines inside of a plane? What were they thinking at *CaliAIR*? To add to that, what kind of name was *CaliAIR*? What is *Cali*? Is it California? If so, where did *Cali*

ome from? *Cali*fornia I guess. And *AIR*? Is *AIR* an abbreviation for airline?
[h]at is a dumb abbreviation. *CaliAIR- Cali* for California, *AIR* for airline. It
s still a very dumb name. Back to my original point, no proper human being
[s]hould ever have to even come into contact with any type of any ungodly
machine? Whether the machine is a telly, a computational device, a cash
egister, or even a radiation chamber (an object otherwise known as a
microwave), no one should ever be forced at any point in their lives to ever
ouch any of those machines. We are not robots, they are. The Ottomans fell
o the Greeks, but it seemed more likely the Ottomans would fall to
machines. Machines are idiotic and have absolutely no purpose in the
modern world of 2092! Machines will one day take down a city, and then a
country. Machines will rule a country one day, and all because some dumb
cashier could not muster up the brain power to count up the money one
person had used to purchase his monthly groceries! All because one person
did something idiotic. That is why I will never, in my right mind use any
type of any ungodly machine in my life, no matter how desperate the
situation. If it means that I will die, then I will have to live (die) with that
fact.

Meanwhile, as I retched at the very sight of those ungodly machines,
Austin No-Last-Name-Because-He-Does-Not-Know-For-Some-Reason was
playing a game on that telly machine thingy. It was a game with a snake
made of cubes that had to absorb smaller cubes on the screen and then grow
bigger but it could not touch its own tail because reasons. It was such the
time-wasting, idiotic, horridly designed, crappy game that Austin was very

221

good at and actually seemed to somewhat enjoy. Austin seemed to just somewhat enjoy that very time-wasting, idiotic, horridly designed, crappy game for some time-wasting, idiotic, horridly designed, crappy reason. He was indeed very obviously good at the time-wasting, idiotic, horridly designed, crappy game. He kept on moving the rigidly-drawn snake back and forth until it *absoorbed* the tiny cube and the snake grew. He only lost one time, and that was when his snake was so large that it took up every single last pixel on the screen, the snake could not move without touching its own body.

Austin offered for me to play, and I politely declined a number of times. I will never touch a machine in my life. Anyways, Austin and I had many interesting conversations about many things.

It was about halfway through the eighteen hour long flight when Austin started an actual conversation, "What identity will you use in Funafuti, Tuvalu once we get there? Despite it being a very isolated country, I am pretty sure that they will know about the entire collapse of the Neo-Ottoman Empire and the rise of the New Greek Empire, since it happened not too long ago, and the event literally changed what the world map looks like."

"I think I will continue to use my Soviet/Russian Nozdryova Lisenka Kirillovna identity, it is an easier identity to keep up than a newer one. I will have to create a backstory." I turned towards him, "You can help me! We need things to do on the nine hours left on the trip to Tuvalu."

"Well, Nozdryova Lisenka Kirillovna is obviously of Russian/Soviet descent, so maybe you should use the story you made up for Gennadiya Petrov but alter it. Nozdryova Lisenka Kirillovna is a Russian/Siberian refugee who disliked the Taiwanese Dynasty's politics and escaped to Tuvalu to escape society," Austin suggested, like a child.

"That works, and I guess that is an entirely plausible scenario in which one would actually escape and flee to Tuvalu from Angelo. Here is a very serious question for once we actually get to the safehaven of Tuvalu," I said, taking a deep breath since I had talked so much. I was truly acting like a Russian/Siberian vagrant who disliked everything about politics.

"Go ahead."

"Once we finally get to Tuvalu, shall we escape again and go on an adventure to other safehavens? Maybe Niue? Maybe Nauru? If you do not want to, then I still would. I have always dreamed on going an adventure between safehavens. It would literally be a dream come true."

"First off, Nauru is abandoned entirely. Also, Niue has a government that is entirely run by a weird cult. We could still go to like New Caledonia or somewhere proper. New Caledonia has an airport."

"Nauru has an airport. We could still land there."

"We would have to hijack a plane," Austin said, seeming naive and absolutely confused at my idea.

I looked at him with a look that I hoped indicate that he was being confusing, "Okay then. New Caledonia is still an option, but it is just too developed. France still owns it and that is not like that fact is going to

223

change by the time we get there. Plus, the Neo-French Empire was one of the biggest allies of the Neo-Ottoman Empire, so they would love to reinstitute me as the new ruler of the Neo-Ottoman Empire version number two."

"So I guess New Caledonia is off of the list for countries to escape to?"

"Yes."

The conversation ended awkwardly. New Caledonia is a territory of the Neo-French Empire, and they would take me back to Europe. New Caledonia has a lot of airports, so if I ever get stuck in New Caledonia, I could take a plane ride out of there without any trouble. I have decided, after lots of deliberation that I would still go to Nauru and Niue despite their obvious problems. Nauru is absolutely uninhabited, and Niue has a government that is led by a cult. Maybe living alone on a completely uninhabited island would not be so bad. It would almost be like an island paradise in a way. Plus, there would never be any ungodly machines in Nauru. If the island is uninhabited, no machines will reside there.

I believe that whether or not Austin or any other people join me, I will have an adventure throughout the Pacific Ocean, from island to island, country to country, it would be quite the life. There are just a few hours left

n my flight, so I decided to grab a newspaper article instead of using any
ne of the countless ungodly stupid telly game-playing machines.

I have attached the article below.

The Neo-French Empire and the German Empire are working together to restore the Neo-Ottoman Empire

Many people nowadays know about the Maurie Osman scandal. Maurie Osman was the heir to the throne of the Neo-Ottoman Empire and was *killed* last December after an unrivaled invasion by the Golden Dawn rebellion forces. Her mansion was destroyed, and her father, and sultan of the Neo-Ottoman Empire, Izzet Osman, was killed within the hour. Izzet Osman's mansion was decimated as well.

About six days after that, the New Greek Empire established who its rightful new ruler was. Dimos Vassallos was first in line, yet Dimos Vassallos was killed during the end of his speech. Qamar Gabris, who was on the stage with Dimos Vassallos, was the natural heir. Qamar Gabris was shot within three seconds of Dimos Vassallos, but by a different protestor. After that, the shooters of Dimos Vassallos and Qamar Gabris were identified. Maurie Osman had shot Dimos Vassallos, yet she identified herself as Gennadiya Petrov, a Georgian refugee. Maurie Osman was actually alive after all. Gennadiya Petrov, or Maurie Osman, was put into solitary confinement when she was found with a gun. Maurie Osman later escaped using a knife that was stupidly provided to her by her guard on duty, Shegan, who was promptly fired.

Maurie Osman's location is unknown, yet she was last seen wearing a red fez and stereotypical Neo-Ottoman "peasant" clothes. While no person has found Maurie Osman yet, two empires are set out to. The German Empire and the Neo-French Empire are each other's biggest allies. The two powerful empires have dedicated a large portion of their budget to finding Maurie Osman, and with her, re-establishing the Neo-Ottoman Empire. The investment made into the search was a joint investment by the two empires, the German Empire and the Neo-French Empire contributed the same amount to the fund. Across the globe, the two empires will search for Maurie Osman in any possible place or area she could be in.

The search is starting in two areas, The United States of America and Eastern Europe. It is suspected that Maurie Osman has escaped to Eastern Europe because of its somewhat Neo-Ottoman influenced culture. The cities of Minsk, Sarajevo, Leningrad, and even Helsinki have been put on a short list of cities Maurie Osman is suspected to be in. Based on her past, it is likely that Maurie Osman has run off to a very highly developed city, hence why all of the cities on the Eastern European short list are major cities of some tier.

In The United States of America, volunteer searches by local German and French populations have already started. Instead of branching out politically to The United States of America, the German Empire and the Neo-French Empire have decided to inspire their local populations to start searching, as a symbol for pride in their community. Some minor Ottoman, Neo-Ottoman and Turkish populations have begun search parties as well. In most of the north and central states, German search parties have grown to an extensive level already. In the far southeast and Far East, French populations are joining in by conducting search parties. In southern Illinois and the far northern parts of California, Turkish and Ottoman and Neo-Ottoman populations have been inspired and started their own search parties. This means that the volunteer search parties in The United States of America is covering almost every last bit of America so far, and it has not cost a penny.

The next locations to be instituted with numerous search parties are Western Europe and Central America. In Western Europe, the empires will be able to carry out search parties everywhere, as they are the two most influential countries in the area. One city that may require extra work is Andorra Le Vella, considering that the local Andorran population hates the Neo-French Empire solely based on the two countries' histories with each other.

In Central America, the German Empire is looking to start recruiting task forces from The United States of America to search for Maurie Osman in Central America and possibly even Canada. It is unlikely Maurie Osman is in Canada, as Canada lacks the presence of even one major or developed city in all of its vast land. The Neo-French Empire is reluctant on the plan, as they are "Worried about spending too much money in the campaign too early," o quote the president of the Neo-French Empire, udovic Boudet.

Will Maurie Osman be found? Will the Neo-)ttoman Empire be re-established and brought back :o its proper glory? It all depends on just where laurie Osman is hiding.

Well, the German Empire and the Neo-French Empire were never ;oing to find me, especially not in a developed or major city. Based on /laurie Osman's past, she would not be hiding in a developed or major city? t is a good thing the media and the public are equally idiotic. I am going a)lace that is anything but developed. I do not criticize their idea to start in :astern Europe, to be honest, if I was a stereotypical Neo-Ottoman heir to he throne refugee that had killed the Neo-Ottoman Empire, I would)robably hide in enemy territory, so probably the very major and developed :ity of Leningrad, which is owned by the Taiwanese Dynasty. Alas, I am not /our stereotypical Neo-Ottoman heir to the throne refugee that had killed the Neo-Ottoman Empire, and I have chosen to take refuge in one of the only)laces no one has ever really heard of: Tuvalu.

It is a shame that I can no longer help the German Empire or the Neo-French Empire. When I was a young lass, I could help my father as he went and helped the German Empire and the Neo-French Empire. He would donate money and supplies and even share war strategies. It is quite a shame that those two empires will totally and absolutely collapse without a "crutch" empire to lean on. The Neo-Ottoman Empire was a simple crutch to them. I never considered the Neo-French Empire or the German Empire as a real empire.

Anyways, I do wonder if they will ever even think to look for me in the middle of the Pacific Ocean. I am not even sure if the German Empire's government or the Neo-French Empire's government has ever even heard of the country of Tuvalu. Those idjits.

The pilot just made an announcement, and the speakers on this *American* plane are LOUD.

We will be landing in Funafuti, Tuvalu in less than one hour. We hope you have enjoyed your flight so far on CaliAIR!

CaliAIR is still a dumb name for a Californian airline.

I have landed. I am in Funafuti, Tuvalu. I have traveled from Istanbul, the Neo-Ottoman Empire to Sarajevo, The Bosnian Kingdom to Angelo, the United States of America to Funafuti, Tuvalu. I am in the middle of the Pacific Ocean. Society does not exist here. Nothing exists here except for a peaceful civilization of friendly people, or at least I hope. I will not know until I actually step foot into my destiny. I will soon step foot into the rest of my future.

I am worried.

The grass crunched with a satisfying sound. It was summer in uvalu, and it always was apparently. With global warming and their lready amazing climate, Tuvalu has one season: summer. There were hildren playing on the airport roads meant for airplanes, it was clearly a ommon open space. Before we landed, they had to sound an alarm so eople who happened to be using the airplane track could have time to move ut of the way. Tuvalu's government is already very nice to its citizens from hat I can tell so far in Tuvalu.

The wind blew with a cool breeze, and it rustled the trees. verything in this country so far makes me feel like it is my home. The irport itself was a light baby blue house shaped building, not anything at all i any way at all like the Angelo airport in The United States of America. he people were incredibly welcoming once we landed, and most people in uvalu so far speak fluent English. I truly feel like this country is one nterconnected family, and the actual land is every single citizen's home. I ope to join the population of this home.

I can not believe I got here. I have escaped society. For once, for one noment, for the first time in my life, I was able to enjoy my life without esponsibilities. Once we landed, we went to see if people actually played n the airplane roads. They do. Austin and I played with the fun children, or no reason! We had no reason at all! It was the first real fun I have ever ad. We are really just tossing a ball around, but everyone finds it so enjoyable in Tuvalu. We met a twelve-year-old and her parents. Her parents were so kind that they invited us on a tour of the "greatest island in the entire world" for no other reason than to see me, a complete and utter stranger to their family smile and be happy in Tuvalu.

First we went to the restaurant streets, a span of streets in Funafuti entirely filled with restaurants. Although all of the fine establishments used to be very touristy, they are all now locally owned and operated. The Plantation Restaurant has evolved since the early twenty-first century. Where a touristy, classy, fancy-schmancy place used to sit, an authentic Tuvaluan grill stands. The family who bought out The Plantation decided to keep the name. Other restaurants like that that changed their ownership and style but no their name are Blue Ocean and Halavai. These establishments have changed everything about themselves except their odd names, is that not peculiar? It was good to have real food, although I have grown to who I am on only meal and snack tubes and juices, I prefer real food.

Next, we went to all of the *important* buildings. We went to the bank, the island supermarket, one of the few convenience stores, most of the many churches, most of the many hotels, and the actual federal government building.

The National Bank of Tuvalu is built with the some home-like fashion as the airport. Most buildings here look like shabby houses, and I am not saying that is a bad thing in any way. The bank allowed for me to exchange bills into other currencies without the hassle of dealing with any ngodly machines at all. I have exchanged all of my remaining money into Tuvaluan currency.

The supermarket in Tuvalu is known as "The Island Supermarket," which is correct considering that it is actually the only supermarket in the country of Tuvalu. People come from all around in Tuvalu just to visit this surprisingly reasonably-priced supermarket.

The convenience store is much more than just a convenience store. They sell more varieties of food than most of the restaurants, although most of the food they sell is pre-packaged, it is incredible. You can buy almost anything there. To add to everything already amazing about the convenience store, every single item sold there is absolutely dirt cheap.

The churches are less than impressive, yet they *get the job done*. There are many of them, and they are everywhere. It is somewhat disconcerting to see a church or chapel every block or so.

The hotels are all very luxurious to a certain extent. Most of them are run by local families, not giant corporations. I was able to rent an apartment in the Funafuti Lagoon Hotel for me and Austin for the rest of both of our lives. I got the largest room available. The hotel has complimentary things, such as complimentary food. There are even outdoor dining tables, and they even have miniature Tuvaluan stick flags on the tables at the hotel!

The federal government building also had a home-like vibe, yet it was bright yellow on the exterior, which was hilarious to see. I dared not to go inside, as I have learned to fear government. Finally on our tour, we went to the beach. We did not do anything much, we just sat there, thinking. I thought about my future and who I had become throughout this adventure.

Where I was once a hackneyed, lackadaisical misanthrope, I have newfound, utile, clairvoyance to add to the abstruse sapience I had, and it is because I have found this brigadoon called Tuvalu. Yes, I have found an English dictionary in one of the libraries and skimmed through it. Tuvalu is a brigadoon and a safehaven, and it truly is a secluded paradise. Here, in Tuvalu, there are almost no problems. You will never hear of someone glomming in Tuvalu. The government is NOT corrupt, it is perfect. While they may not have a high revenue, or even a revenue that can match my net worth, they make use of what they have. They host community events weekly. Overall, it is like one giant family in Tuvalu.

Now, everything is perfect. I can be at peace. I do not have to worry about politics, I do not have to worry about upkeep for a positive image in the media, I do not have to worry about my father, I do not have to worry about my safety, I do not even have to worry about my future. I know that what will come is what will come, it is not like anything bad could happen in Tuvalu.

I can not wait for my future. I can not wait for my future in Tuvalu. I can not wait for my future in Tuvalu with Austin.

Chapter Nineteen

Tuvalu is amazing. I am in Funafuti, and I have been enjoying Tuvalu since the second Maurie and I landed. I do not know where to start with Tuvalu, it is just so amazing. We landed and heard a loud blaring noise right before. When we asked the pilot what it was, they said that it was an alarm to alert the people who were playing on the airplane roads. I did not believe him, and nor did Maurie. As soon as we landed, we went out and looked at the airplane runways. There was no way kids could be doing this, but then again, there was no other place to use as a park in Tuvalu. There were a bunch of kids tossing a ball around, having fun. Upon seeing us stare at them like creepy people, they invited us to play with them. We just tossed the ball around and actually had fun. Everyone was laughing and it was truly a magical moment. I immediately forgot all of my worries and concerns, and just focused on the moment. This is where I will spend the rest of my life, so I should enjoy it here. Just doing nothing can be relaxing, and it made me feel like I was part of something for once.

Whilst we played that random ball game, we met a nice twelve-year-old-girl, who realized we were not citizens of Tuvalu and invited us to her house. We accepted the gesture and went over. Her family was very generous and wanted to welcome us into Tuvalu. They offered to give a tour of the island, and Maurie and I accepted graciously. First we went to restaurants, as both Maurie and I were absolutely starving after the very long plane ride. The restaurants in Tuvalu have real food, and it is amazing. I have grown accustomed to meal and snack tubes and juices, but real food is so much better than consolidated, barely-flavored nutrient tubes. We scarfed some traditional Tuvaluan cuisine down, we continued. I can not even remember what I had, I was having just that much enjoyment in that specific moment.

Then we went to all of the important places in Tuvalu, all of the places we would need to know about. We went to the bank, the island supermarket, one of the few convenience stores, most of the many churches, most of the many hotels, and the actual federal government building.

The bank was first, and it was weird. It was very busy, with people streaming in and out constantly. The maintenance was poor, yet everyone there was happy with it. I converted all of the small amount of money I actually have left over to Tuvaluan currency, so I can use it all in Tuvalu. The bank tellers were the kindest people I have ever met. Strangely, there were no ATM machines in the bank at all. In The National Bank of Tuvalu, you would expect there to be at least one measly ATM so that customers could easily convert their money in a timely manner.

The island supermarket was appropriately named "The Island Supermarket," and it was the only supermarket on the island. It is a large and flat building. Many things there cost less than they do in The United States of America. It was interesting to see the local brands, rather than the international brands and companies I was used to seeing on convenience store and supermarket shelves. While we were there, we bought some basic

ood needs, which consisted of only real food. They do not have any meal or
snack tubes or juices in Tuvalu.

The convenience store we went to was remarkable. First off, it had
more food than most of the restaurants had, and had unusual foods, like *fried
chicken*! Second off, there was everything you could ever need, including
toiletries, clothes, food, things needed in houses (mugs, tables, etc.), and
many, many commodities and trinkets. I bought a mug for a beverage I
learned about called *tea*. Tea is very popular in Tuvalu because of its British
heritage, or at least that is what the cashier told me when I asked him what
he tea bags at the front were. Basically, you put a mix of herbs pre-
packaged in a bag into boiling hot water and mix. Then, you wait for it to
cool and maybe add a sweetener and mix the beverage again. We will soon
come back to that convenience store to buy toiletries and more commodities.

The family took us to many churches. It was disconcerting seeing a
church every mile or so on the street. There are churches and chapels all
across Tuvalu. It is weird to see so many for a person who has seen one or
two in their lifetime so far.

Next, we went to hotels to try and find a place for Maurie and me to
stay. The first hotel was too expensive, the second was too shabby for
Maurie, and the third was just fine. We got the largest room available in the
hotel and settled in briefly. There are two beds, two tables, a shelf of books,
and two bathrooms. It is a very luxurious place, it feels almost like a
mansion or a palace. The hotel had complimentary food in the lobby areas.

They even had outdoor dining places. The tables outside had little miniature Tuvaluan stick flags on them, it was great!

Finally in this segment of the tour, we went to the federal government building of Tuvalu. It was humongous! And it was all yellow! It was a very attention-grabbing building. It was beautifully built and it was amazingly maintained. There was not much to do there in the tour.

For the final segment of the tour, we went to the beach. We just sat down on the beach and chatted. The family is very nice and it seems that I have already made friends in Tuvalu. I was able to tell them about my adventure, and they seemed impressed by how much I had gone through just to get to Tuvalu. I noticed that Maurie was isolating, she was off in another part of the beach, just staring out into the ocean. I decided not to bother her.

It is amazing in Tuvalu so far and I can not wait for my future. I can not wait for my future in Tuvalu. I can not wait for my future in Tuvalu with Maurie, or should I say Nozdryova Lisenka Kirillovna.

We have fully settled into the small apartment in Tuvalu. The room is basically split into two sections, so we each get one. I let her have the better side. We are at the family's house, and we are learning about the culture of Tuvalu. The family's name, as we have found out, is Hamblin, and they originally lived in Australia, and it shows in their accents. The ather, Carter Hamblin, showed us how to make the boiling water herb infused beverage.

First, you put what is known as a kettle on the stove and turn the stove all the way up. I had never even seen a stove and now I know how to properly use one! You wait until the water comes to its boiling point two-hundred-twelve degrees Fahrenheit or one-hundred degrees Celsius. Once the water has fully boiled, you pour the insanely hot water into mugs. In those mugs, you place a tea bag.

Tea bags were not used until 1908, before then, families would own large chunks of herbs that you would chip off of and place in a strainer to infuse. I learned that from the mother, Sienna Hamblin as the water was slowly boiling. A New Yorker by the name of Thomas Sullivan first started shipping tea bags worldwide, although patents and ideas had already circulated in 1904 and 1903.

Once you have placed the tea bag in the boiling hot water, you can add sugar or some other sweetener, like honey, to add to the taste. After that, you wait. You have to wait a long time before tea is at a proper temperature to even drink without burning yourself. Tea tastes amazing. Especially fruity and citrus teas, I know this for a fact, as I have had about seventeen cups of tea so far. Every cup of tea tastes better than the last. I like honey in my tea, and of all of the teas that I absolutely love, which is all of them, I like orange citrus tea the best. Maurie has stated that she does not like the taste, and would prefer coffee. She said that she has gone too long without having a proper cup of coffee.

After hearing this, the Hamblin family took us out to a local restaurant again to have coffee and tea and biscuits. I had about seventeen more cups of wonderful tea, and discovered that I do NOT like minty tea. Carter Hamblin, the father, had a cup of tea sweetened with something called Stevia, and showed Maurie and I what *biscuits* were. Biscuits are a type of real food similar to bread, except crunchy and thin like a chip. People will top these concoctions with butter and jam, similar to how one may top toast regularly. Sienna Hamblin had some overly-sweetened coffee and by overly-sweetened, I mean she put eight packets of sugar in, and then added just about seventeen tablespoons of honey. It was like that the coffee was barely even coffee any more. Maurie had a cup of black coffee and tried a biscuit, which she enjoyed greatly. She seemed relieved that she was finally able to have a cup of coffee once again, even though it was not the famous Turkish coffee.

Maurie was very thankful for them taking us out for drinks, and kindly paid the bill. I have realized, after spending some more time with Maurie Osman, that she is filthy rich. She bought one month of the apartment's rent up-front, without having to withdraw more cash. She has a consistent supply of what most people would say is an excessive amount of currency at any given time. Finally, she is constantly buying very expensive things. She buys the fanciest and most "natural" of all of the toiletries available. It is sometimes frustrating to see a level of wealth being used that I can not obtain. I think that Maurie Osman, in terms of her net worth, has more money than the entire federal government of the country of Tuvalu.

Her wealth and her social status are very impressive to a regular person, such as me. I am back at the hotel/apartment building now, and I am writing. I am surprised at how well things in Tuvalu are going so far. I expected there to be a hiccup, or a problem of some sort.

I awoke to a knock on the hotel door. The knock rang throughout the room and bounced off of the walls, and it landed in Maurie's and my ears with a sharp pang. I awoke immediately. Maurie rolled over. What a princess she is. I was startled and stumbled to the door, still in my newly-cheaply bought pajamas. I opened the door and was greeted by a German man who appeared to be the same age as me. He was wearing a heavy jacket, which was inappropriate for the Tuvaluan climate, "skinny" jeans, and an oversized bright brown beanie. Beneath the beanie lay choppy and sloppy blonde hair and a sly grin on his head.

"Hello," the man said in a light and high German accent, "I am from next-door, and I would like to know my new neighbors," he stuck out his lanky hand for me to shake, seeming overly-amiable for the time of morning that it was.

I was dazed from my sleep, or thereof lack of, and stuck my hand out despite that, "Hello," I said, as my voice cracked from my dehydration, "I

241

am Austin, and my roommate is Nozdryova Lisenka Kirillovna, or Noz for short. Thank you for checking in on me, what is your name?"

"Well hello, Austin," he pronounced it *Aughstien*, "and hello Noz," he shouted towards Maurie, yet he pronounced it *Nogshh*, "My name is Oskar Blattner, and I moved in here two weeks ago, for a," he stuttered and glanced away at the cloudless sky, "a-a business trip. I am glad that I have new neighbors to share the wonders of the country of Tuvalu with."

"Well thank you again checking in on us, it is very nice to have another friend in Tuvalu. Would you like to join us this morning for breakfast at this wondrous apartment building?"

"Well, sure. I will try. I will try." Oskar Blattner then walked away from the door as fast as he had come to the door.

That was odd. Very odd. I was hoping that breakfast would be somewhat pleasant, although, Oskar Blattner, did not seem like the nicest person. I do not think he would be the greatest person to have as a friend in Tuvalu. Maurie awoke as soon as Oskar Blattner left, she hopped up from the bed and ran over to me, looking more dazed than I was.

"Who was that?" she mumbled.

"Oskar Blattner, our apartment neighbors, I invited him over to breakfast with us this morning."

"So a German fellow came with no background and you invited him over to have breakfast with us?"

"We are in Tuvalu, how could anyone be mean?"

"You are absolutely brilliant," Maurie said facetiously

I rolled my eyes, and she walked away towards her bed, but she continued to talk, "Did you tell him my name was Nozdryova Lisenka Kirillovna, and not Maurie Osman?" Maurie asked.

"I am not that naive."

Maurie and I sat down at the table, across from Oskar Blattner. He was dressed the same as when he was at the door. Once we sat down, he already seemed antsy. He was squirming in his tiny, German clothes, and it concerned Maurie and me, but we colloquially decided not to mention that through a very thorough moment or two of eye contact. We sat down in the plastic chairs and looked at the menu. They had lots of options for breakfast. The apartment building had so many options for breakfast that I was unprepared!

Oskar looked towards us, and realized we had come, yet he did not look pleased, "Hello! It is wonderful to see you here! Shall we order? I would truly recommend the fish toast, as it is very common to eat a fish dish or fish of some denomination for a breakfast in Tuvalu."

243

I repositioned myself in the chair, squeamishly, and continued the conversation, "That sounds delicious. How are you doing this fine morning?" I asked, knowing that he would crack.

He was uncomfortable, yet he resumed the conversation, clearly and obviously bothered by my question, "I am doing just fine," his German accented voice lost its normal sense of cheeriness, "How are you?"

I stared him down, as he nervously tapped his foot quietly, "I am doing great. How are you doing, Nozdryova?" I turned to Maurie, hoping to normalize the odd conversation.

The tension between Oskar and I continued to build. He was clearly nervous, and he clearly had something that he was worried about. "Fine," Maurie said, clearly not wanting to get involved. She continued the conversation and tried to reroute it, "For an icebreaker, what languages do you speak, Oskar?"

Oskar looked relieved the conversation was going somewhere, "I speak English, as you can tell, German, French, and Turkish. What languages do you speak, Noz?" he eased back in his chair.

Maurie looked nervous, as if she may reveal who she really was by knowing so many languages, "I speak German, English, as you can tell, and Bosnian, which I learned for the sole purpose of getting through Sarajevo's airport on the way here to Tuvalu on the flight."

"Well I speak German, Hmong, Vietnamese, and English, as you can tell," I quickly responded, not wanting to leave any space between responses which tensions between all of us could rise without regular conversation to help us avoid tensions from building.

"That is impressive, where did you come from again, Minnesota?"

"Yes."

"I could tell by the languages you spoke."

"Ok."

Awkward silence filled the outdoors atmosphere. Everyone at other tables continued chatting away, loudly. Maybe it was only loud since no one at the table I was at was talking. Oskar shuffled around. Maurie looked gloomy. I just sat there, not knowing what to even do. I was excited at least to try Tuvaluan breakfast cuisine for the first time ever. Only a few minutes passed, about four and a half, yet it felt like a few hours. I tapped my fingers rhythmically on the table, waiting patiently for anything at all to happen at the table.

"May I take your orders?"

Oskar was standing in the doorway, as he waved goodbye. "It was fun having breakfast with you." He left as soon as he could, just as he had done last time he was there.

I turned to Maurie, "That was weird."

Maurie ran over and closed the door, "Indubitably, and he seems like he has something to hide."

"That was obvious."

"What could he be doing?"

"He did not look or sound like he was capable of doing much anything," I laughed heartily.

"That is true, yet we can not trust anyone."

"Why not?"

"Because I am," she switched to a very quiet whisper, "Maurie Osman, and many governments are looking for me."

"Oskar Blattner came to Tuvalu weeks before we did, there is no way he could have known you were going to be here, that is impossible," I lowered my voice to a similar quiet whisper.

"He was from Germany. They could have tracked me." Maurie seemed to be very noticeably worried.

"Calm down, there is no way he could have tracked you."

"Fine. You are right."

She calmed down and she was mostly fine for the rest of the day. Although she held in some anxiety, she was able to function throughout the day. Despite this hiccup, in the form of a horrible neighbor, my future in Tuvalu will still be amazing. I still can not wait for my future.

Chapter Twenty

It has been four and a half months since I last wrote in this journal. I am on a German Warship on the way to Brisbane, Australia. I did not prepare for this.

One and a half months ago, Oskar Blattner introduced us to his "cousin," Dominic Blattner. Dominic Blattner sported the same clothes of Oskar Blattner, yet had a worse attitude. He was also thirty or so years older than Oskar, yet still was Oskar's apparent "cousin." He was very nonchalant about how much he hated us, yet it is now apparent to us. His cousin had come from the Taiwanese Dynasty to escape his own society, and came to Tuvalu because of his "cousin's" recommendations about Tuvalu. He was nice at first, and moved in with Oskar. He barely ever came out of the apartment; he isolated himself consistently.

Then, one day, Dominic invited Austin and me to dinner with Oskar. At that dinner, Dominic started asking us countless questions. He asked who we were, where we were from, why we came to Tuvalu, when we came to Tuvalu, how we came to Tuvalu, who are families are, and what we intended to do in Tuvalu. Mind you, he had barely said a word or two to Austin and me before this dinner. As soon as we sat down, Dominic attacked us with many, many, personal questions. Oskar just sat there, writing down our answers under the table on a notepad, yet he was not doing a very good job of hiding his writing of everything we were saying.

That was when we started to stray away from hanging out with Oskar Blattner or Dominic Blattner. They seemed to start to notice this, as we had avoided them constantly, and they invited us to even more events. They invited us to "parties" that never really happened and dinners no one showed up for. We continued to gradually move away from them.

Two weeks later, they invited us on a "cruise" to Australia. We politely declined the offer. There was a scheduled cruise ship to Brisbane in the Tuvaluan news, but we no longer trusted Oskar Blattner or Dominic Blattner. When they asked us why, we said that we did not want to go to Australia. Honestly, we really did not want to ever go back to society, much less the society of Australia. They were quite offended, and very angry at us.

Two days ago, a German warship visited unexpectedly. Normally, German ships only visit Samoa, or American Samoa, yet there was now a giant German warship at the shore of Tuvalu. The warship was enormous, it was even larger than most commercial cruise ships. There was a commander on board, who docked the ship and left his crew on the ship. He came down from the deck to visit Tuvalu, and he went down right towards me. By then, a large crowd had congregated by the Funafuti shore, watching the giant German warship dock.

I was in the near back of the interminably sized crowd. Despite me being barely visible to one who was onlooking the crowd from the deck of the giant German warship, the commander passed through everyone just to

248

et to me. He pushed by people who were asking him why he was here, the ommander even pushed past a government representative from Tuvalu. He topped at me, and grabbed me by the shoulder. Everyone who saw gasped. will remember that moment and exactly what he said forever.

"Hello Nozdryova Lisenka Kirillovna. Come with me."

Austin tagged along, of course. He stated that he could "help me." Yeah right. He can not even hijack a plane. He was just ruining his own future; he had sealed his own horrible fate. The crowd physically tried to top him from taking Nozdryova Lisenka Kirillovna, as we knew almost everyone on the island at that point. Honestly, it was quite impressive how many new friendships in Tuvalu we made. It was wonderful. I did not try to top Austin from coming, but he said that it would be helpful to have a friend. Maybe he was right.

The commander introduced himself as Sir. Detlev Loewe to Austin and me. He went straight to the federal office with us, making sure that we were guarded by his bodyguards at all times. Before we left, and before the bodyguards were there, we went back on the deck and gathered the bodyguards and some supplies. Halfway through the oddly long walk to the federal government office, he offered us each a snack tube. It had been so long since I saw a snack tube that I did not even remember what they were. I got a cracker flavored snack tube. It tasted like raw dough with an excess amount of salt in it. Austin clearly did not like his snack tube either. I still very much prefer real food to food tubes or food juices. However, Sir. Detlev Loewe seemed to enjoy his snack tube greatly.

He dragged Austin and me to the front desk and demanded to speak to the person of the highest power available. Luckily, since Tuvalu is never really up to anything, the Tuvaluan president is always free. He was not very happy to meet Sir. Detlev Loewe, as he was the Northern Directive Administrator of Special Services of Germany. Sir. Detlev Loewe's job consisted of funding and administering special tasks and services in the specific northern region of Germany. He is the one who came up with the initiative to find me. I hate him. Unfortunately, although he is the Northern Directive Administrator of Special Services of Germany, Sir. Detlev Loewe is also the Southern Directive Administrator of Special Services of Germany, as he is filling in Erika Scholl, who died recently. He is planning to merge his two jobs together and become the Directive Administrator of Special Services of Germany, and not the Northern Directive Administrator of Special Services of Germany or the Southern Directive Administrator of Special Services of Germany. It is an initiative which he is orchestrating, which is just one of the many examples of how the German Empire's government allows government officers to misuse their power.

Anyways, Sir. Detlev Loewe spoke to the Tuvaluan president very harshly and rudely, and with no respect whatsoever. It was a horror to watch. He demanded that I, Nozdryova Lisenka Kirillovna, should be taken

250

way and forcibly removed from the country of Tuvalu. The Tuvaluan president, Vincent John, disagreed with this order, obviously. He kindly asked for Sir. Detlev Loewe to leave Austin and me in Tuvalu and for him to return to his ship. Sir. Detlev Loewe did not follow through with these orders, and was then, somehow positively and politely, threatened by Vincent John to an excessive extent.

Sir. Detlev Loewe did not back down. That was when he revealed who I really was to the Tuvaluan president. At first, Vincent John did not believe Sir. Detlev Loewe. Then, he looked at a published picture of Maurie Osman, and then back at me. He then realized that Sir. Detlev Loewe was absolutely right. He asked me if I was indeed Maurie Osman, and I, of course, said that I really was not. He did not believe me. Vincent John then asked for Austin and I to leave the specific room, and we were escorted out by the bodyguards.

Whilst we were outside of the room, we overheard Vincent John and Sir. Detlev Loewe discussing the treaty made between the Neo-French Empire and the German Empire. We also overheard Sir. Detlev Loewe try and bribe Vincent John with thousands of dollars for him to let Maurie Osman, me, to get into the hands of the government of the German Empire. Vincent John, despite his strong morals, succumbed to his request and accepted the bribe.

We were invited back into the room, and as soon as we step foot into the Vincent John's room, Austin stupidly told Vincent John that he had heard them discussing a bribe for thousands of dollars. Vincent John denied this claim, and so did Sir. Detlev Loewe. Eventually, they admitted to it, but only after a long and hard argument that involved a large amount of yelling. Vincent John's official statement at the meeting was: "That is none of your business." Sir. Detlev Loewe's official statement at the meeting was: "That is just how government works nowadays. I am just doing what works to do what I am required to do."

I hate Sir. Detlev Loewe. So does Austin, I hope. We were led by Sir. Detlev Loewe's bodyguards back to the giant German warship. I could not believe this was happening. Just as I had found a safehaven, a brigadoon, I was taken away from it. How had they found me? I had covered up who I really was, but maybe I had not covered up what I looked like enough. I am honestly impressed by the efforts of the government of the German Empire.

Nozdryova Lisenka Kirillovna and Gennadiya Petrov were both Russian/Soviet/Siberian identities, maybe that was the first lead. Maybe they tracked my passage from Istanbul, which would have been impossible, unless the taxi driver had told the government. I can not even remember if I told the taxi driver about anything important. They did get one thing right. The first place I went was Sarajevo, which is indeed a major city.

Ali Ertugrul and Yuce Catli were hired to place a gun with me and get me into solitary confinement in exchange for them getting free from prison. I had told Ali Ertugrul AND Yuce Catli about Tuvalu, I told them about my plans for traveling to a safehaven, and I even showed them a Tuvaluan coin. I can not believe I made the mistake of telling people where was going. It is obvious how the German Empire's government found me, hey simply asked Ali Ertugrul and Yuce Catli if I had said anything about ;oing somewhere after prison. I can not believe I had fallen into the trap of naking friends, that is why you must never trust anyone, even if they seem ike they are trustworthy and they like you. Never trust anyone. Ever.

I wonder where Ali and Yuce are now. If the German Empire was asily able to contact them both, then neither of them are in the New Greek impire. Where had they gone? Perhaps they had gone to Hamburg, the only najor city within the German Empire, they seemed like the kind of people vho might do that. Heck, they could be on the ship waiting to see the precise look on my face the exact moment I am taken away from Tuvalu and ent off to Germany.

I trudged through the sandy beaches, next to Austin. We both held pur heads down, and went in the exact directions we were told. The crowds :hat had gathered to see the ship parted themselves as we passed through, not daring to mutter a single word. The Tuvaluan president, Vincent John, who had sealed my fate was trudging along with us, talking to Sir. Detlev Loewe about something called the "Arctic Reconciliation." I was not in the mood to ask about the news. Vincent John did not seem unhappy that we had been banished, he seemed to not care at all. Sir. Detlev Loewe did also not seem to care at all, as one would have thought.

I kicked the sand, depressed. I had travelled all the way here, yet had only been taken right back to society. I had failed myself. I had failed. Austin had failed. It was my fault that Austin had failed. I had ruined everything. I had ruined everything not only for me, but for Austin as well.

It was a long walk back to the German warship. I walked through the streets of Tuvalu for the last time. I tried to memorize what everything in Tuvalu looked like. I tried to memorize what the restaurants were called, and which were the best. I tried to memorize all the people Austin and I had met. We had met the Hamblins, they were the first people we had met. We met Leon Kane, who had strong political beliefs that I agreed with. We met Dylan Morgan, who had also escaped society and gone to Tuvalu, he had come from northwestern Serbia. I can not list everyone who Austin and I met, or I would be here all day. Despite my self-proclaimed antisocial attitudes and behaviors, I was able to make a new social life for myself in Tuvalu.

Everyone in the crowd waved goodbye, looking at us with eyes worn from tears. Maybe they realized that no president, no matter of what country, should send off one of its residents to a horrible place. It was a sad sight. Austin and I slowly boarded the German warship, taking the most time we could with each possible step. We wanted to be in the country of Tuvalu for as long as we could, even if we were only in Tuvalu for the length of three footsteps longer.

The warship was colossal. It was taller than most buildings in Tuvalu, and almost as wide as half of the island itself. To say that German

254

warship was only colossal is an understatement. It was the largest ship in the world. I could hear Sir. Detlev Loewe bragging about it to Vincent John. Once we got to the entrance of the warship, or one of the entrances to the warship, Sir. Detlev Loewe had to say goodbye to Vincent John, and after a combined time with each other of less than one measly hour, it still seemed as though Sir. Detlev Loewe and Vincent John had somehow made friends with each other as they sent us off to Germany.

Austin and I entered the warship, followed by the various German guards and political figures. This was the point of no return. We would have to go back to our lives, back to society as we know it, and we would never, ever see Tuvalu or any of its residents ever again. The governments the German Empire, the Neo-French Empire, the Bosnian Kingdom would make sure of that for me. Austin may be released into the middle of Germany, sent to make a life for himself instead of returning to the life he had in Eden Prairie, Minnesota. No one would care about who Austin was and if he would go back to Tuvalu. Austin may just be able to escape back to Tuvalu again, as long as he goes completely unnoticed by the Tuvaluan president, Vincent John, when he arrives back in Tuvalu.

Inside the ship, it was pitch black.

Sir. Detlev Loewe lost the smile he held on his face from meeting Vincent John, he reached towards something, and come up with an old and dusty lantern. He held it above all of our heads, "Follow me."

255

We followed Sir. Detlev Loewe in the darkness. It seemed like he absolutely knew where he was going. I reached my left hand out. My left hand was greeted with a metallic *clang*. That was a steel wall. I reached my right hand out. My right hand was greeted with the head of the guard assigned to me. I recoiled away from him, disgusted that I had just touched him in the darkness. I continued to follow Sir. Detlev Loewe down the steel corridor. The guards' boots clanked against the metal loudly. I could not wait to get out of that corridor and into the real warship interior itself. The metal corridor was cramped, uncomfortable, and smelled foul.

The walk through the corridor took a long time. It was odd. Besides the excessive smell of the place, the corridor was entirely dark except for the tiniest bit that was illuminated by the lantern that Sir. Detlev Loewe was carrying. You could everyone in the corridor slowly breathing. I believe that that interminably long metal corridor drove me insane.

Finally, we arrived at a door. It was a metallic door. Sir. Detlev Loewe handed off his lantern to the nearest bodyguard, the one assigned to me, the one who I had accidently touched. The lantern illuminated his face. He had light brown hair that drooped over his eyes, green eyes so bright that they illuminated themselves, a small nose, and a smaller mouth. Sir. Detlev Loewe knocked on the metallic door harshly, as if he was attacking it.

A random face appeared through a rectangular slot in the middle of the door, all we could see were its eyes, "What is the password?"

Sir. Detlev Loewe sighed, "The password is das kennwort."

The door slid open loudly. I walked into the room. It was a mostly wooden control room with wooden doors off to the sides, leading to other rooms in the ship. As I later found out, the door on the left led to the regular living quarters. That is where Austin, me, and the bodyguards live. It is hard sharing a room, no matter how very expansive it is, with that many people. Considering how wide the room is, it would not have been much trouble to put in barriers. The room itself is wider than seventeen rooms combined together. Like the warship itself, it is absolutely colossal. I guess the Germans have very high living standards.

The door to the right has the professional living quarters. That room is where political figures on the ship like Sir. Detlev Loewe live. That room, as I have found out, is twice as wide and is twice as long as the regular living quarters. Currently, it only provides residence to a few political figures. That is an excessive amount of room for a small amount of people.

In the rest of the ship, there are two more control rooms, and two common meeting areas. The control rooms are extra, they are used to read the news and things like that, so no one ever really goes into those rooms.

The first common area is a meeting area. The second common area is a dining hall, where we are required to be at certain times of the day.

At 8:30 AM in German time, they make us go to the room to have breakfast. But before that, they make us wake up at 7:50. At 11:45, they take us there for a small snack, which is odd. Do they have to watch us eat? At 1:30, they take us to have lunch. At 4:00, they take us to the second common area for a second snack. At 6:45, they take us to the second common area to have dinner and dessert. The food on the ship is less than admirable. It is mostly meal and snack juices for snacks, and for meals it is mostly meal tubes and/or juices.

I have met my personal bodyguard, or the bodyguard who was actually assigned to me. His name is Fabio Vahlen. Austin has a personal bodyguard as well, and her name is Gina Knacke. Neither of the bodyguards are particularly friendly to Austin or me. It is not fun spending every second with them.

Anyways, Sir. Detlev Loewe sat down once we got into the main control room. He sat down in a handmade wooden chair that looked too amazing to sit in. One man sat down next to him. They conversed briefly in German. They talked about who Austin was, and why he was here. They looked up a record on him on one of the ungodly machines that they had in he ungodly main control room. The ungodly main control room was filled o the brim with ungodly machines.

The record popped up, and it showed almost nothing. He was born in Austin, Texas in the United States of America in 2070. His full name was ust Austin. Even on his official file, Austin had no last name. How odd. It dlso showed his gender, age, height, weight, and jobs. He had two jobs in wo different cities before he escaped to Tuvalu. Finally, it said "Location: Jnknown". Sir. Detlev Loewe made sure to fix that. He put in where we vere going. Apparently, we are going from Funafuti, Tuvalu to Brisbane, Australia to Newcastle, Australia to Keelung, the Taiwanese Dynasty to Moscow, the Taiwanese Dynasty to Hamburg, the German Empire. Then, ve would settle this whole political mess in Hamburg.

After his conversation regarding Austin had finished, he held down a small green button. A dial tone played.

Eventually, someone accepted the call, "Hello?"

"We found Maurie Osman."

Made in the USA
Columbia, SC
14 January 2019